More Praise For
James S. Gardner's
Dark Continent Chronicles

"I highly recommend The Lion Killer. *I have seldom come across such fine descriptive writing in a thriller."*
—*James Patterson,*
America's Best-Selling author

"A riveting thriller with twists and turns galore."

—*Robert Halmi, Jr., Emmy and Golden Globe Award winner,*
Executive Producer of "Lonesome Dove"

"Few really good books come out of Africa, but James Gardner's 'The Lion Killer' is one of those few. It's easy to see that Gardner has been there and that he understood what he saw. His powerful writing illuminates the Dark Continent."
—*Nelson DeMille,*
New York Times *best-selling author*

"James Gardner has done it again and more so! His first thriller was captivating. This one is riveting. An excellent read!"
—*Charles and Barbara Whitfield,*
Best-Selling authors

"Sara and I were blown out of our chairs by the power of your presentation and we wish you a whole lot of luck with 'The Lion Killer'!"

—*Barry Farber,*
national talk radio host

"The Lion Killer is an extraordinary read on an extraordinary mission. For those that actually consider the future of Africa, it may very well change their perspective."

—*Douglas Harrington,*
Hamptons.com

"The book is certainly 'write what you know'. Gardner has been to Africa 25 times...Gardner's passion was contagious."

—*Lee Fryd,*
The New York Resident

"Gardner's story-telling approach follows in the path of Dashiell Hammett: 'Life is disposable; the Land is beautiful and the search is fatal.'"

—*James Edstrom,*
Times Square Gossip

"In this book, James Gardner takes you on a thrill ride through so many terrifying places and events in darkest Africa, you have to pull the covers over your head to finish it.

Hell of a trip for us adventure readers!"

—*Dan Jenkins,*
Novelist & Journalist

James Gardner

THE HONEY GUIDE

DARK CONTINENT CHRONICLES BOOK III

JAMES GARDNER

PENNINGTON PUBLISHERS

JAMES GARDNER

PENNINGTON PUBLISHERS
ISBN 978-1-935827-19-1
Trade Paperback
© Copyright 2013 James Gardner
All Rights Reserved

Requests for information should be sent to
the following websites or email addresses:

JamesGardnerNow.Blogspot.com
DarkContinentChronicles.Wordpress.com
JamesGardnerNow@Gmail.com

Pennington Publishers and the Pennington logo
are imprints of Pennington Publishers, Inc.

Cover design: Donald Brennan / YakRider Media
Interior design: Donald Brennan / YakRider Media

Printed in the U.S.A.
Also available on Kindle

FOR LIAM, ANDERSON AND BARBARA GRACE

ACKNOWLEDGEMENTS

I would like to thank my editors: R.C. Knutsen, Barbara Gardner and Lynn Denney. I owe special gratitude to my publisher, Donald Brennan.

James Gardner

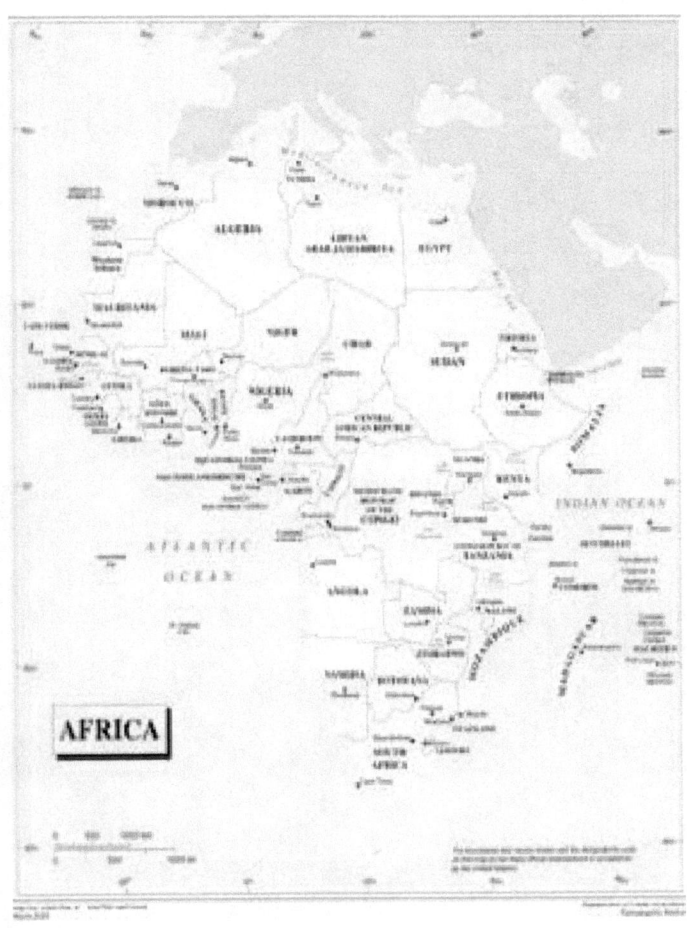

JAMES GARDNER

The Honeyguide

The African black-throated honeyguide is an ordinary looking bird, but it's far more cunning than most living things. Honeyguides lay their eggs in the nests of other bird species. After the hatchlings kill their nest mates, they consume the food foraged by their new parents. When food is scarce the ravenous chicks sometimes eat the parents.

A symbiotic relationship exists between honeyguides and the tribes of southern Africa. The bird leads honey gatherers to wild beehives. As payment, pieces of the hive are left for the birds to eat. Bushmen believe that if no payment is left, the honeyguide will take revenge by leading the honey collectors into the path of a hungry lion.

JAMES GARDNER

Prologue
Brooklyn

The director yelled, "Quiet, please! Lights and reflectors, primary close-up, rolling, action!" A gaffer snapped the clapperboard. A makeup artist dusted the man's face and then stepped out of view. The news commentator pasted on his camera-face, raised a microphone to his lips, cleared his throat and waited for the red light. "I'm standing in front of a deserted grocery store in Bedford Stuyvesant. On the September 11, the television commentator, Sean Mahoney, and Rigby Croxford, a citizen of Zimbabwe, were abducted in broad daylight in the middle of Manhattan. They were blindfolded by armed kidnappers and driven to this location."

The director switched to a secondary camera panning the store's interior.

"The victims were imprisoned in this meat locker."

The camera focused on two wooden chairs equipped with restraining straps. "What took place in this horror chamber was reminiscent of Medieval Europe. Were these men abducted by foreign operatives working under the direction of the Chinese government? Was the kidnapping orchestrated by one of New York's most prominent divorce attorneys? When we return, the answers to these questions and more. We're back after a word from our sponsors."

"Cut."

1

Hong Kong
One month earlier

The one-hundred meter yacht, The Honeyguide, rode at anchor in a quiet bay cradled in the arms of Hong Kong. Oceangoing junks with furled sails bobbed alongside as fishermen filled wire baskets lowered from the ship's galley with yellowfin tuna and live crayfish. Smaller sampans offloaded fresh produce and flowers. When the wake from a Macau ferry jostled the boats, the captains shouted insults.

One of the Honeyguide's four Hinckley tenders idled up to her stern. The launch was returning from a roundtrip to the downtown wharf. Onboard was the American cable television reporter, Sean Mahoney.

As they waited for mooring lines to be tossed down, Sean noticed two men armed with machine pistols staring down at him from the pilothouse. Before the tender could be secured, a cabin boy scrambled onboard and grabbed his suitcase. Sean followed the boy up the gangway. He was confronted by armed guards. One man rummaged through his suitcase while the other man frisked him. Satisfied, they directed him to the spiral stairs leading to the upper level. He sidestepped deckhands block-sanding the teak decks. Sean would learn that they were erasing high-heel shoe dentations from the previous night's cocktail reception honoring the Russian ambassador.

The cabin boy opened the door and stepped back. Sean's stateroom opened onto a railed balcony with a panoramic view of Hong Kong's skyline. A fruit basket and a bottle of 1982 Chateau Mouton sat on an antique desk. The accompanying note read: Welcome aboard. Nelson Chang. Sean rubbed his eyes and yawned. As he tested the bed, the telephone rang.

"Good afternoon, Mr. Mahoney. After you freshen up, Mr. Chang will receive you in his private quarters. A steward will present himself momentarily. If there's anything you require, please call. We have staff on duty around the clock. Pleasure, sir."

The steward wore a crisp blue business suit. Sean followed him down a passageway that opened into a grand salon. The burled walls glistened like Stradivarius violins. Sean recognized paintings by Mapplethorpe and Monet. A cylindrical glass case displayed a Ming Dynasty vase. A matching case exhibited a Faberge` egg. A male receptionist stood up and bowed. "Good morning, Mr. Mahoney. Mr. Chang is waiting for you in his office. You're free to take notes, but recording devices are not permitted at this time."

[2]

Sean followed him into a dimly lit foyer. He opened the door for Sean and stepped back. The office décor was French. The chilled air smelled like jasmine. Nelson Chang wore a white linen suit and matching gloves. He was looking through a porthole with his back turned.

"Good morning, Mr. Mahoney. Can I offer you a cup of coffee or perhaps tea?" Chang watched a sampan beating against an offshore wind. The mainsail was a grimy patchwork. Her unpainted gunnels were stained by feces and rust.

"I trust you found the accommodations acceptable?"

"Incredible. Fit for a king, in fact."

Chang pointed. "I grew up on a fishing-junk like that one."

"Tea would be great. On behalf of my network, I'd like to thank you for granting me this interview. Your yacht's magnificent. I was wondering about the name?"

"I consider myself an amateur ornithologist. The honeyguide is a bird found in southern Africa."

"Well, I must say, I'm impressed."

Chang ignored his compliment. "How long have you worked in the television business?" He turned around and stuck out his hand. His grip was firmer than Sean had expected.

Sean was shocked by his appearance. He knew Chang had been involved in a helicopter crash, but nothing prepared him for seeing the man in person. His face was devoid of eyebrows and lashes. His left ear was rimless. Glossy scars caused his facial skin to droop. The centerpiece of his face was a piercing black eye, like the hieroglyphic eye on an Egyptian sarcophagus. His other eye was covered by a white patch.

Sean stammered. "Almost t-t-t-twenty years."

[3]

"Oh dear, I hope I haven't frightened you. I'm afraid I have a similar effect on most people who see me for the first time."

"No sir," Sean said unconvincingly.

"You're asking yourself why I haven't had plastic surgery. Obviously, I can afford the best surgeons in the world. Truth is, I've undergone ten major operations. It was, as you can imagine, a terrible accident. That's why I wear these." Chang held up his gloved hands.

"Where was I. Oh yes, what college did you attend?"

"Yale."

"And your major?"

"Middle Eastern affairs."

"Do you speak Arabic?" Chang asked.

"*Na'am.*" Sean sensed Chang already knew the answers to the questions he was asking.

Chang diverted to faultless Arabic. "Tell me about yourself, Mr. Mahoney."

"I thought I came here to interview you, not the other way around," Sean said using English.

Chang looked at him with an icy stare. "So, I divulge my innermost secrets and you remain anonymous. If you think that's the way it works with me, I'm afraid you're sadly mistaken. I stopped being dictated to a long time ago."

"Fair enough. Ask me anything you want."

"Are you married?"

Sean's eyes implied despondency. "As of right now, I'm separated."

"I'd say this is your second or third marriage. Probably a much younger wife this time around. And that she asked you for a divorce. Am I right?"

Sean felt his face redden. "My first wife died. Kathy was, or rather is, my second wife. I'd say our separation was mutually agreed to."

"You needn't be embarrassed about being rejected by a younger woman. What's important is that I trust you implicitly. To gain my trust, you must be totally honest with me. Now, did your wife ask you for the divorce or not?" Chang stood up indicating that if Sean's answer was unacceptable, the interview was over.

Sean hesitated momentarily. "My wife asked for the divorce."

"Very good, Mr. Mahoney. A man's eyes can be a roadmap to the truth."

Sean started to say something, but resentment succumbed to curiosity. *This is the strangest man I've ever met. And besides, Harry will shit if I come back empty-handed,* he thought.

"Now then, Mr. Mahoney, I'm sure your legal department has briefed you on our contractual arrangement. As you know, I reserve the right of editorial review. That's why we're doing the interview here with my camera crew. I can assure you, the equipment's top-of-the-line. It's not that I don't trust you, it's just that I don't like surprises."

"I understand, completely. I was wondering about why you finally agreed to be interviewed."

"If you've done your homework, and I assume you have, you know I was in the arms exporting business. Now, I'm a consultant for China's sovereign funds, which are currently over four trillion dollars. As such, I'm making investments all over the world. Some countries are nervous about China's emergence as the next economic superpower. By doing this interview, I hope to soften my public persona. Newspaper cartoonists in your country have caricaturized me as a bucktoothed, yellow devil with a forked tail." He pushed out his upper teeth and hissed through them. "As you can see —the teeth maybe, but not even the slightest evidence of a tail. It's not unlike how your newspapers depicted the Japanese during the last world war."

"What's our time frame?" Sean asked trying unsuccessfully not to grin.

"This is an abbreviated outline of my *curriculum vitae*." He pushed a manila folder across his desk. "I'll give you, say, one hour to review it. We can discuss your proposed queries over lunch."

"Just one question before I go. I know you went to Oxford and then Harvard Medical School. Your entrance scores were the highest scores ever recorded. I'm curious, Why did you drop out of medical school after two years?"

"I wasn't interested in devoting my life to healing. I know that sounds rather simplistic, but it's an honest answer."

"Sir, your English is perfect. How did that come about?"

"English preparatory schools. My classmates literally beat the accent out of me. And majoring in linguistics at Oxford didn't hurt."

"Children can be cruel."

"They can, indeed."

"How many languages do you speak?" Sean asked, trying to verify what he'd read.

"Eight. By the way, I don't have an accent in any of them. It's all in there." Chang pointed at the folder. "Now, if you'll excuse me, I have business to attend to."

Chang stood up and bowed.   Sean watched him disappear down the passageway.

After Sean was alone in his stateroom, he scribbled down the following facts taken from Nelson Chang's CV:

Nelson Chang: born 1939, Nanking, China
Mother: Lu Chang. Father unknown
Grew up on a fishing sampan
Mother died when he was 14
Adopted by the English couple,
Mr. and Mrs. Robert Bridges, of Manchester, England
Moved to Great Britain 1955
Private schools in England.
Graduated Oxford with high honors
Harvard Medical College. Dropped out after 2 years
Owned Trident Exports for 30 years
Consultant for China's sovereign funds

Sean reviewed the questions he planned to ask Chang. Lost in concentration. he picked up his pen and tapped his teeth like he working on a crossword puzzle. He closed his eyes and dozed off.

When he woke up he was anxious about missing the meeting, but his catnap had only lasted a few minutes.

One hour later, Sean was ushered into the dining salon. Chang motioned for him to sit down. A waiter pulled back his chair as another man placed a laced napkin in his lap. A wine steward wearing white gloves stepped forward with a bottle of red wine in one hand

and a bottle of white in the other. Sean indicated his selection. The man poured a small amount of wine and waited for his approval, which Sean gave without tasting.

"Your art collection's incredible. Ever worry about the humidity?"

"They're not reproductions, if that's your inference. How did you find the reading?"

He was shocked by Chang's clairvoyance. It took a few seconds to recapture his thoughts. "You've led an interesting life."

"Interesting to some people, I suppose, boring to others. Now then, let's review your proposed questions."

"I read someplace that you're one of the wealthiest men in the world. Exactly how wealthy *are* you? As a part of that question, how much does the Chinese Government pay you for managing the sovereign funds?"

"To tell you the truth, I haven't the foggiest idea concerning my net worth. Americans are obsessed by wealth. I must tell you, I find that a rather repugnant trait of Americana. As far as my consulting work, I receive one dollar per year for services rendered. Obviously, my motivation isn't monetary."

"In all of the articles written about you, one central theme stands out—your criticism of the United States."

Chang fidgeted uneasily. It was clear he didn't like the question.

"Your country hasn't been very kind to me. Over the years, I've acquired substantial personal holdings in America. Some of your country's more vocal politicians say I shouldn't be allowed to invest in your key industries. They say I'm a threat to your national security. Of course, they enthusiastically accept my campaign donations. Now that I'm managing China's sovereign funds, those same politicians are, shall I say, more cordially inclined towards me. China is currently holding one trillion dollars of your country's debt. Need I say, more?"

"You say you're only a consultant, but the people I've talked to say you manage China's sovereign funds like it was your own money."

"I have had a certain degree of success. I think the powers-to-be are satisfied with my performance."

"To digress, I'd like to discuss your history as an arms dealer. I read someplace where you brokered a controversial deal between the United States and China." Sean paused, referring to his notes. "I'm talking about the transaction that involved selling secret encryption technology."

Chang acted like he didn't hear the question by hijacking the conversation in another direction. "The United States has used China as a buffer against Russian aggression for fifty years. Russia's implosion has made that foreign policy rather obsolete, wouldn't you say. Let's move on, or we may never eat our lunch."

"Any regrets about supplying weapons to some of the world's most despicable regimes?"

"You know what they say. One man's terrorist is another man's freedom fighter. Mr. Mahoney, I can't count the number of times I was paid by your country to sell arms to subversive groups. It was a symbiotic relationship. And a very profitable one, I might add."

"I'll take that as a 'no apologies' answer."

"None, whatsoever," Chang reiterated.

"You were quoted as saying, 'America will end up as a footnote in world history'. Can you expand on that thought? Or simply stated, do you think your antagonistic rhetoric is the reason you've received such unflattering press in my country?"

"I'm not sure I used those exact words. The epicenter of man's universe has been New York. Before New York, it was London and before London it was Paris. You could argue that the center was in Berlin for a brief time in the thirties and maybe Tokyo in the early seventies, but basically, the United States has been the engine driving the world's economy and everything else for that matter. Throughout history all great empires eventually fail. It happened to the Romans and more recently to the British Empire. Why, if it weren't for North Sea oil, England would be the economic equivalent of Greece."

Chang leaned forward and brought his hands together. "Take your country. America has become a land of obese people sitting in front of their televisions collecting money they didn't earn paid to them by the very politicians they keep electing. And yes, I know that's a gross generalization, but indulge me while I make my comparison. In contrast, China currently has twenty-seven million students enrolled in engineering and technical schools. You're graduating lawyers and forensic accountants. You think you can litigate yourselves to prosperity. Within a few years most of the remaining manufacturing industries you take for granted will move to China. Why? Labor's cheaper here and the Chinese people are exceptional workers. It's pure Darwinism and it's a *fait accompli*. Beijing will become the new epicenter of the universe."

"You're depressing me." Sean swished wine in his glass and sniffed it. He watched the droplets slide down.

"I don't know why. It's just natural selection. Someday, Beijing will fold her tent and the epicenter will move again. Stay tuned, Mr. Mahoney, The world's forever changing."

"The countries that have challenged America's innovative spirit haven't fared too well. The Japanese come to mind."

"This time we're talking about China's enormous population. It's a numbers game."

"Some people believe that war's inevitable between our two countries."

"America's got her hands tied with a billion-plus Muslims. It's like two retarded children fighting over the color of their imaginary dog. The ignorance is beyond belief. If I were a betting man, I'd say that the next major conflict will be between India and China fighting for economic dominance. And look, I'm talking about fifty years from now. That last comment was strictly off the record."

"Yes, of course." Sean's mind filled with rebuttals, none of them worth the price he might pay for expressing them. "Now that I've got your vision of a new world order, I'd like to ask you a few personal questions. You say your mother was a peasant and that you were born in Nanking in 1939. Wasn't that around the time of the Japanese invasion?"

Chang fell silent for a few long moments. He fished a monocle from his breast pocket, scrutinized some invisible speck and then polished the lens with his napkin. His dark malignant eye turned as resolute as a hawk's. Sean felt a chill run down his spine.

"Let's not beat around the bush, as you say in your country. Why don't you ask the real question you want answered?"

"Which is?"

"Am I half Japanese? I am taller and much better-looking than most Chinese men." Chang laughed self-mockingly, but his eye told a different story.

Sean was at a loss for words by Chang's shift away from his ice-cold formality. He regained the moment by stating, "Part of this documentary *is* a human interest story. You said you wanted to soften your public image. To do that, we need to make you more than a billionaire ex-arms dealer."

"*Touché*, Mr. Mahoney. My mother told me that I have 51 Japanese fathers. That's how many soldiers in the Imperial Japanese Army raped her. She said there was so much semen running down her legs it filled up her shoes. She was one of the 80,000 women raped in the invasion. Fortunately for me, she wasn't one of the 260,000 peasants massacred."

Sean sighed. "I'm sorry I asked the question." A tiny stab of regret touched his heart.

Chang's face revealed he took pleasure in making Sean uncomfortable. He softened his discourse by adding, "I don't know why. We can't alter our past, no matter how ugly it might be." Chang permitted himself a rare smile, but the humor faded in a flash.

"Your mother died when you were still a child. Was she sick for a long time?"

Sean waited for Chang's elaboration. When he realized none was forthcoming, he asked, "Could you comment on the English couple who adopted you?"

Chang motioned to the steward to start serving lunch. He rose from the table and walked over to the same porthole. He spoke in a hushed clinical tone with his back turned. "Do you know anything about bipolar disorder? His eye was closed now. "The depression is debilitating.

I'm not talking about being down in the dumps. I mean living on the edge of insanity. The fear of falling into the abyss and not being able to climb out."

After looking into his wine glass for a long moment, Sean blurted, "Is it like schizophrenia?"

Chang spun around. His empty eye socket twitched. He steadied the eye hole with his hand and tried to speak, but a coughing jag delayed him. Deep rattling came from the depths of his lungs. He covered his mouth with a napkin and ejaculated phlegm into it.

"There's no similarity." Chang daubed his lower lip daintily "In fact, there's linkage between mood disorders and intelligence. Experts say that Hemingway and Isaac Newton had the illness. In a number of cases, the afflicted have advanced mathematical abilities. Other sufferers might have advanced language skills. If a person's gifted in one discipline, he or she is sometimes deficient in the other."

"A mathematical genius who has trouble reading," said Sean.

"Precisely. In some cases, the individuals have both abilities. Imagine what it's like to remember everything you've ever read or heard."

"A photographic memory," said Sean.

There was no doubt that Chang was describing himself. Sean noticed Chang's lower lip quiver. The look in his eye revealed that his mind was someplace far away.

"It must be a wonderful advantage in life."

"It's been an absolute curse. Memory can be one of the greatest blights inflicted on the human race. It's not only the good things you remember. It's the dark secrets normal people bury in their psyches. Fortunately, I've developed a decoding method. Without medication, I'm sure I'd be locked up in a lunatic asylum or worse.

Let me give you a demonstration. Give me your birthday, just the day and the month will do."

"The fourth of January," replied Sean.

"All right, here goes. On the fourth of January, the following historical events occurred.

In 46 B.C., Titus defeated Julius Caesar in the Battle of Ruspina.

247 B.C., Saint Eutychian became the Pope.

1493, Columbus left the New World on his voyage back to Spain.

1642, King Charles had ten members of the English Parliament arrested.

1717, the Netherlands, England and France signed the Triple Alliance.

1725, Benjamin Franklin arrived in London.

1885, Dr. Grant performs the first appendectomy.

1896, Utah was admitted as the 45th state.

Now, give me a three digit number, any number will do."

"How about 453?"

"The square root of 453 is 21.2837967. I could give you more, but I think you get the picture."

Sean shook his head in amazement. "My God, you really are a genius."

"What I do is cerebral calisthenics. It doesn't require grand mental acuity."

"Modesty becomes you, Mr. Chang."

Chang ignored his compliment. "Sadly, the other symptom is social alienation. Throughout my life, I've had problems relating to people. Sometimes I make insensitive remarks. It's not that I mean to hurt people—

it just happens. You asked about the couple who adopted me. I was homeless and starving when they took me in. Amazing what a human being will do to survive. I won't ruin your lunch by giving you the sordid details."

The recollection flushed his jaundiced complexion. He regained his composure. "As I was saying, they raised me like I was the son they never had. I owe them everything. After I left Manchester and moved to Boston to enter medical school, I never saw them again."

"But why?" Sean said.

"A family reunion would have been too upsetting for them, and me. For years, I tried to express my affection for my parents, but I could never pull it off successfully. In my defense, I did take care of them financially. They lived out their lives as millionaires on a rolling English estate. It was the least I could do."

Chang had opened the door; Sean knew he had to step through it carefully. "It's wonderful, I mean, what you did for them."

Chang's long speech had left him winded. Instead of answering, he acknowledged the compliment by raising his wine glass. Chang inconspicuously extracted a pill from a golden pill box and popped it into his mouth.

"I was about to ask why you never got married."

"The idea of having a woman under foot has always repulsed me." When Chang saw Sean's reaction, he added, "Having a man around would be even worse."

They chatted over their Chilean sea bass. Sean was seduced by Chang allowing him to see his inner being. Chang had exposed his underbelly, which made him seem almost likeable. Sean scribbled in his notebook as he worked up the courage to ask the question that would be the focus of the documentary. Here goes, he thought.

"I'd like to get your assessment of China's role in the terrorist activities plaguing Africa. I'm referring to the bombing of the American embassies in Kenya and Tanzania. And what's happening in the Sudan? I've heard rumors that China knew about the terrorist attacks against American interests before they occurred and chose not to warn the United States. Those same sources say China's purpose is to frustrate America's influence on the African continent."

Chang looked at him with an eye as sharp as a dagger. "Why, that's absurd. Your country has pillaged Africa's resources for two hundred years. America leaves nothing in her wake but scorched earth." He held up his hand to prevent Sean's response. "That was a bit harsh. Maybe we should strike that one."

"Consider it stricken. Now then, as a board member of the Chinese Petroleum Corporation, I'm interested in getting your view concerning China's role in securing oil concessions in Africa. Specifically, some people say China's promoting ethnic violence in the Sudan. Is this part of a plan to lock up the drilling rights in the Darfur region? Is China partially responsible for, well, the killing of 400,000 indigenous Africans?"

"When you say 'some people', of course you're referring to the Americans again. It's no secret that China's economic future is tied to Africa. Seventy percent of the world's strategic minerals and huge oil reserves make it so. Spreading vicious lies won't stop us. In truth, we're helping Africans all over the continent, including those living in the Darfur region, I might add. What did the Europeans or the Americans ever do for Africa, besides promote slavery?"

"What about trillions in foreign aid?" Sean asked.

"And what happened to it? The living standard for Africans is lower now than it was fifty years ago. Your sister's a bigwig in African politics, why don't you ask her?"

Sean considered Chang's suggestion. His sister, Helen, had told him on more than one occasion that China was devouring Africa like a locust outbreak. He decided against referencing his sister. "Sir, how can you defend genocide?"

Chang stood up abruptly and walked back to the same porthole where he stared at a freighter heading out to sea. His voice sounded unassailable this time. "I believe the number of deaths you just stated is grossly exaggerated. The world is beleaguered by zealots. The problem in the Sudan is religious fanaticism, not China."

"Care to comment on your country's investment in Sudan's oil infrastructure? I've heard it's over ten billion. As part of that question, why does China have 4,000 soldiers stationed in Khartoum?

Chang motioned to his cameraman to stop filming. He spoke sharply without turning around. "I'm confused. I thought you wanted my vision of China's economic future. Let's finish our discussion tomorrow."

"I'm afraid that's impossible. My flight leaves tonight."

"I took the liberty of canceling your reservations. My private jet will fly you back to New York. I knew we'd never conclude our business in one day. I hope you approve."

"It seems extravagant."

Chang turned back. "Extravagance is what I do best. Surely, your producer won't fire you for missing one day."

Sean held up a finger giving him time to swallow. "I just need to call New York."

"Good, then it's settled. After we finish our work, I'm taking you to the racetrack. I have a horse running in the last race. After dinner, I'd like to give you a taste of Hong Kong's nightlife."

"It sounds tempting."

"Oscar Wilde once said, 'I can resist anything, but...?'" Chang challenged Sean to finish the quotation.

"Temptation."

"Very good. Can I call you Sean?"

"Of course."

"I like to be called Nelson. My parents named me after the English flag officer, Vice Admiral Horatio Nelson. Thank God, they didn't name me Horatio. I guess it's only apropos that I live on a boat."

"I'd hardly call this a boat." Sean opened his arms expansively. "It's more of a cruise ship."

Chang acknowledged the accolade with a courteous nod. "I'm sure you'll find the evening, shall I say, amusing. Let's leave around four. Hong Kong's traffic is appalling. No city planning by our ousted British landlords. Until this afternoon," he said, shaking hands.

2

At four o'clock sharp, Chang and Sean were escorted to the helipad on the Honeyguide's fantail. After helping Chang and Sean up into the helicopter's backseat, Chang's bodyguards climbed in behind them. The twin engine Sikorsky lifted off, dipped its nose and banked for the short flight to Hong Kong's downtown heliport.

Victoria Harbor was crowded with anchored ships. Sampans and sailing junks crisscrossed the harbor. The helicopter's flight path took them directly over a sampan. A woman squatted over the side. She wiped herself with a fistful of newspaper and then waved to them as they passed overhead. At the stern, her husband dipped a bucket of water. Chang guessed the man would wash the fish they would eat for their dinner. Probably boiled rockfish and cabbage, he mused. As Chang explained the incident, he smiled when he saw Sean grimace. "Perhaps it's not the meek that shall inherit the earth, but the more resilient."

The helicopter turned back into the wind, hovered momentarily, and then landed on a skyscraper. The elevator ride ended in a subterranean garage. A uniformed chauffer standing beside a stretch Rolls opened the door for Chang, who deferred to Sean.

The Queen's highway was hazed by exhaust flatulence spewing from cars and trucks. An ant-like procession of bicycles lined both sides of the road. Sometimes, the Rolls passed so close, Sean couldn't believe the riders' cone-shaped hats weren't blown off. Their chauffeur veered to the shoulder giving a motorbike room to pass. Sean clinched his fists as he watched the motorbike narrowly miss an oncoming bus.

"Phew!" Sean gasped. "That was too close for comfort."

Chang explained, "Hong Kong's citizens are the most law-abiding people in the world. Unfortunately, our traffic laws are seen only as suggestions." The rest of the drive wasn't as breathtaking.

The car turned off the highway. The sign read:

Royal Hong Kong Racing Clubhouse
Members Only

When they exited the Rolls, the clubhouse attendants descended on them like blowflies on raw meat. Sean felt the prying eyes of the crowd as he followed Chang to his private box.

"I hope you're as pleased as I am. I'm referring to the interview." Chang handed his cane to a waiter.

"That was the easy part. Now the real work begins. I mean with the editing. Vodka, straight up," Sean said to a waiter.

"I'd like the 1998 Opus from my private bin." Chang spoke in Mandarin and then switched back to English. "Sean, are you sure you wouldn't prefer wine? Opus really is God's nectar."

"Make mine the same."

Chang handed him a racing program. "My filly, Typhoon is running in the tenth."

"Where do I bet?" Sean got up. "I'd like to place a bet if you think she has a chance."

"Relax, Sean, I've got you covered."

"Hope you didn't bet too much. Divorce lawyers are killing me."

Chang said, "Drink up, my friend. We've got twenty minutes to post time."

They were escorted to the paddock by Chang's bodyguards. Typhoon was a large chestnut filly with white forelegs and a blazed face. The handler led her out of the stall. She pranced nervously as the trainer helped the jockey mount. After some last minute instructions, Chang brushed the filly's nose for good luck. They returned to Chang's box.

"Don't get confused. Unlike your country, we race horses in a clockwise direction." Chang handed his binoculars to Sean.

Sean licked his lips. "I can't believe this wine, it's incredible."

"It is rather nice, isn't it?" Chang redirected Sean's attention to the starting gate. "They're off."

Typhoon broke poorly. At the halfway pole, she was two lengths off the lead and fading. At the top of the stretch, the jockey released the reins and showed her the whip, but he didn't hit her. The filly changed leads and closed on the other horses like they were Georgia mules.

[21]

Chang watched the race with total indifference. Sean jumped to his feet screaming. Typhoon won the seven furlong sprint by two lengths.

"How much did I win?" Sean asked boorishly. "It can't be that much, not with those odds."

"Well, let's see." Chang stared at the tote board making a mental calculation. He placed a pencil to his lips and said, "It looks like you won... fifty thousand, give or take."

"Not in dollars?" Sean said. Chang nodded.

"You can't be serious. It's too much. I can't possibly accept that much."

"Oh, but I insist. You are in China. You wouldn't want me to lose face, would you?" Chang pulled down the corners of his mouth into a gruesome scowl.

"God knows, I can use it with the divorce and all. Nelson, I can never thank you enough."

"I like to take care of my friends. All I ask for in return is an unbiased documentary."

Sean caught an undetected glimpse of Chang. There was something about this man that unnerved him, but greed trumped his intuition.

3

After dinner, Chang hoisted his wineglass and toasted, "Sean, here's to you and your last night in Hong Kong. I've arranged a very special send-off for you."

"You'll never top today's race."

"Hold the applause. We have places to go and people to meet."

Fu's was located in the Hong Kong's red light district. Madam Fu cackled as she opened the front door. Sean thought it was a nightclub. When he saw scantily dressed women moving in the shadows, he knew otherwise. Madam Fu had seen the last autumn of her sex life. Her face was dusted with alabaster white powder. Ruby red lips outlined yellowed teeth. She wore an oyster blue *qi pas* fastened at her neck and slit up one side. Fu was humped over with crab-like limbs.

She took Sean's arm. "You special VIP, you have good time tonight."

"I don't know about this, Nelson. As I told you, I'm still married."

"There's no harm in getting a great massage. After all, it's an ancient oriental custom. See you soon, my friend. Enjoy yourself."

"You come with me." Fu led Sean down a darkened hallway. She opened a door and gently pushed him in. "Why you look so frightened? Maybe you no like girls. Maybe you sissy-boy."

"Of course, I like girls. It's just that..."

"My girls take good care of you." She closed the door behind him.

Sean heard giggling before his eyes adjusted to the dark. Four girls encircled him. Their hairless bodies were as smooth as Chinese porcelain. Silky black hair fell lazily across their faces. The scene resembled a wreathing tangle of snakes. "I'd like to keep these on." Sean tried unsuccessfully to hold on to his boxers. He felt his pulse rate quicken.

They helped him into a steaming Jacuzzi where they washed him with soft sponges. They brushed their hard nipples against him. When a girl tried to touch his privates, he stopped her, which evoked more giggling. A girl handed him a cup of something, which he gulped down without hesitation. The girls left the room. Sean felt a tingling sensation. He thought about trying to stand up, but his legs felt too rubbery to support him.

After a few more minutes, the girls reappeared. After bathing him, they dried him with warm perfumed towels. Sean still showed no sign of arousal. He tried to conceal himself. One of the girls removed his hands and playfully scolded him. This induced more giggling.

Challenged, the girls increased their efforts. The one with jutting breasts inhaled him into her mouth. He tried to stop her, but his resistance was feeble. One girl brushed her hair across his face. Another presented her nipple to his lips.

When Sean groaned, the girl applied a deep thumb pressure at the base of his testicles, which short-circuited his completion. His legs trembled as they guided him into an ice-cold shower. They pressed their bodies against him for warmth. The ritual was repeated two more times. Each one building in intensity and each time his fulfillment was agonizingly suspended.

Sean was no longer in control. A girl squatted on top of him taking him deep inside her. Two girls sucked on his toes. The fourth lowered herself into his face. The musky smell of her launched a roaring ecstasy. He needed for it to end, but it continued until he thought his heart might burst. When it finally did end, he lay there twitching. Slowly, the lighting improved. A girl handed him a cigarette. His mind cleared. Foreboding fear washed over him.

Deep in the bowels of Madam Fu's bordello, Nelson Chang pursued another vice. He lay naked curled in a fetal position on a pillowed bed. The gurgle from his opium pipe was the only sound. As Madam Fu studied Chang, she wondered why he never let the girls touch him. He was a distant unknowable man. To see him naked filled her mouth with a bilious sour taste. The old woman smiled. She was happy she was too old to work the rooms.

Later the night, Sean climbed into the backseat of Nelson Chang's Rolls. "Well, that was different." He appeared sheepish.

"I must say, you look very relaxed," Chang said.

"As I told you, I'm in the throes of a divorce."

"You're a long way from home and you're among friends."

"Think there's a chance of my catching something?"

"Madam Fu's prostitutes are cleaner than your wife," Chang blurted.

The comparison made Sean bristle, but he kept quiet.

"Tomorrow, after we review the final edit, you can be on your way back home," said Chang

"If you have the time, I'd like to get a Cook's tour of your yacht."

"I have an early meeting with some Arab businessmen. After that, I'm at your disposal."

Chang leaned his head back and adjusted his eye-patch. He had played his cards shrewdly. He now had insurance if the need should ever arise.

4

C hang ordered his captain to give Sean a guided tour of the Honeyguide. They started in the engine room. Bored with staying in port, the South African captain conducted the tour with such unbridled enthusiasm, Sean felt compelled to pay strict attention.

Meanwhile, Chang used an Asian edition of the *London Times* to shade his eyes as he watched his helicopter land and the passengers disembark. This meeting was an irritant for Chang. At first, he declined it, but China had just become the number one oil consumer in the world. As a board member on the Chinese Petroleum Corporation, it was his duty to entertain dignitaries from the Middle East to insure the flow of imported oil.

He took inventory of the passengers. Three Arabs wore flowing white robes and checkered headdresses. They walked behind a corpulent military officer. He was dark-skinned and wore a camouflage uniform, a red ascot and beret. That one's an African, probably from Somalia,

Chang reasoned. And then it dawned on him, he knew the man. He was a general in the Sudanese army. His name was General Muhammad Obon. He watched how the general carried himself. Nothing's changed; you're still a pompous toad.

A steward made the introductions. "Mr. Chang, this is General Muhammad Obon of the Sudanese Army."

Chang stuck out his hand hoping to avoid the traditional Arab greeting. He was unsuccessful. He wiped his cheeks. Chang used fluent Arabic. "The general and I are old friends. Life must be good. I see you've added a few kilos." He pointed at the general's potbelly.

"I am delighted to see you again, Nelson." The general laughed. His belly shook. "I see you've added a few million pounds, yourself." He waved expansively at the yacht. Obon removed his designer sunglasses. Debauchery had inflated his face until his eyes were reduced to slits.

"You gentlemen are?" Chang asked the three men standing behind the general. The spokesman stepped forward saying, "We are only Allah's humble servants."

So, you're unwilling to give me your names, Chang thought. Just as I suspected, you represent some fanatical movement, probably Hezbollah or al-Qaeda.

"What can I do for you?" Chang was visibly irritated.

Before they answered, Chang corrected the man's greeting taken from the Koran. "What you meant to say was, 'In the name of Allah, the Merciful, we are only his humble servants.'"

The Arabs bowed in deference to his command of their Holy Book.

"Can I offer you Champagne?" Chang asked, hoping they would be offended enough to leave. The Arabs appeared stunned by this blasphemy.

"We Chinese indulge ourselves in all of the major vices. What about you, general? Will you join me? It's a Cristal Brut. I believe the vintage is 1990."

"Sir, your Arabic is perfect and you quote the Koran, but you're not a Muslim." The Arab speaking was frowning. The other men shook their heads.

Chang laughed. "My interest in religion is purely intellectual. Now, how about that drink, general?"

"Unlike them, I'm not devout. I will drink with you, my friend. It's been a long time. Mr. Chang sold me arms many years ago." The general added, "I wasn't sure you'd remember me."

Chang thought, how could I forget someone so vulgar? "It's true the general and I did business many years ago and I have the scars to prove it." Chang pointed at his rimless ear.

"Praise Allah, you survived the accident." The general spoke with counterfeited concern pasted on his bloated face.

"You praise Allah. I prefer to praise my surgeons. Back to the reason why you asked for this meeting?" His orchestrated irreverence caused them discomfort, but not enough to make them leave.

*   *   *

At the same time Chang was meeting with the Arabs, Sean was being shown the communications room. All of the yacht's staterooms and salons were monitored by security cameras and microphones. The captain handed Sean a headset. He was so eager to demonstrate the technology that he inadvertently turned up the volume. The captain zoomed in on Chang's meeting. Because what the captain heard was in Arabic, he felt no compulsion to protect the confidentiality of the meeting. Sean understood every word and gave no indication that he was eavesdropping. To divert the captain's attention, he asked an inane question about the electronics. The captain received an urgent message from the bridge. He excused himself and left Sean alone.

*   *   *

The Arabs got into a heated discussion. The general seemed like he was in another world. He wolfed down the Champagne like it was ginger ale. The Arabs pushed the smaller man forward to speak for them. Chang wondered why the man was clean-shaven, but he lost the thought waiting for him to talk.

"I begin in the name of Allah. He is the One who causes life and brings death. "

Yes, yes, in the name of Allah. Get on with it man, Chang thought edgily.

"Only a handful of men know about the glorious day that lies ahead. The general says that you have always supported our cause. Many have died, and more will become martyrs for this, the ultimate fatwa. For years we have tried to purchase an atomic weapon. And now..."

Chang leaned forward and held up his hand to stop him. "There's no need to continue. It's true that I have been a faithful friend to the Arabs. But I'm no longer in the arms business. And even if I were, I could never obtain such a weapon. Men, all of whom shall remain anonymous, have approached me in the past to help them procure such a weapon. Jet fighters and tanks are always available. Obtaining a nuclear weapon, even the miniaturized variety, is something quite different. I'm sorry you've wasted your time, gentlemen."

It took time for them to digest Chang's words. Curiously, they all smiled.

The general spoke first. "Mr. Chang, you're an international financier. How do you think a thermonuclear detonation in the United States would affect the world's financial markets?"

Chang appeared unsettled. "Of course, it would be catastrophic. An economic holocaust might be a better description." They nodded happily.

"Again, I say to you, I have no way of obtaining such a weapon. In the past, I helped you move your financial assets around the world. Each time we eluded your enemies, they made it more difficult. The violent acts you direct against the Americans make them stronger, not weaker. I'm sorry you've wasted your time, gentlemen. Good day," Chang said, standing up.

The Arabs conversed quietly. The larger Arab put his hand on Chang's shoulder. Ignoring the gesture, Chang got up and paced anxiously, hoping they would get the message and leave.

The general smiled benevolently. "With His divine guidance, we have already procured the ultimate weapon."

Chang felt the punch of the words. His pulse quickened. An unsettling silence filled the salon. It seemed like minutes, but it was only seconds before Chang spoke. "Why are you telling me this? Don't you see—delivery of the weapon is equally important." He

[31]

moved uneasily as he internalized the implications. He needed time to think.

"Sir, you have misjudged our reason for seeking your council. The Final Judgment Day is upon us. Praise Allah, we already have the weapon and we know how to thrust it into the belly of the beast."

"Then why do you need me?" Chang asked.

"The Jewish money-lenders have blocked access to our foreign accounts. This is why we are here. If you knew the exact time and date of an atomic attack against America, how much would you be willing to pay us? Before you answer, we may be ignorant men, but we know the world's economies will suffer. China's sovereign funds are at your disposal. I believe the term you used was an 'economic holocaust'. A man with your expertise could make billions with the information we can provide. We must have funding if we are to continue our Holy war."

Chang walked to a porthole and stared out sightlessly. To him, the absurdity of a religious feud embroiling the world in violence was incomprehensible. A serene calmness washed over him. He saw himself as an innocent bystander watching history unravel before him. He glanced at the Arab's reflection in the porthole glass. What will they do if I refuse to help them? Impossible to stop madmen willing to die for a cause, no matter how idiotic, he thought. If they were telling the truth and if he didn't act, China's reserves could be devastated. His mind raced through possible scenarios. What would oil sell for? Would gold double or triple? With four trillion dollars in the sovereign funds there was no way of calculating the losses. Properly handled, the profit potential was enormous. A terrorist attack of this magnitude could accelerate China's ascendancy as the world's new economic juggernaut. More importantly, it would cripple the United States. This wasn't about vengeance; it was about China's destiny. This could be the largest wealth transfer in history. For the time being, I must pretend to believe them.

Chang spoke with his back turned to hide his enthusiasm. "Of course, I would need to substantiate your claim. A fee of say —three-hundred-million dollars is within the realm of possibilities."

The general jumped up and shouted, "In the name of the Exalted One." The other Arabs also jumped to their feet.

Chang pondered the future. Do they know how much violence this will bring down on the Arab world? Retaliation by the United States will be lethal and swift.

Chang looked uncomfortable. Sweat dotted his face. He pulled on his collar for relief. He probed for information by stating, "If we are to proceed with this undertaking, I must know every detail, no matter how insignificant. For instance, I assume it's a suitcase bomb. I need to know the delivery method and the location of the attack. And there's the timetable. I will be taking tremendous financial as well as personal risks. There is much to do."

"Sir, we also have timely preparations. You will have your details." The Arab looked provoked. "You should know the weapon isn't a suitcase bomb. It's a twenty kiloton mega-bomb."

The smaller Arab stood up and embraced Chang. Chang unconsciously wiped his cheeks. "How will I get in touch with you?"

"It's safer if we contact you."

[33]

"People talk. Absolute secrecy is paramount. Lives are at risk," Chang warned.

"For Muslims, life's eternal. You should consider giving your life to Islam, before it's too late."

"I'm afraid it's already too late for me and him." Chang looked at the general, who belched and then covered his mouth. The Arabs shook their heads.

"Allah willing, you will hear from us soon."

"I hope you're not offended, but before we continue, I must see the actual weapon with my own eyes," insisted Chang.

"We will make the necessary arrangements," said the larger Arab and then offered as an afterthought, "We hope you also are not offended. You should know there are countless martyrs willing to sacrifice their lives if what was said here today should be heard by our enemies."

"Your warning is misguided." Chang looked at the general for support.

"This man is like a brother to me." The general slurred his words between hiccups.

"Accept my humble apology." The Arabs bowed.

"Goodbye, Mr. Chang. And may Allah protect you."

5

The following morning Sean and Chang reviewed the interview videotape in the private theater onboard the Honeyguide. Sean was lost in his private thoughts. Normally, Chang would have sensed the change in Sean's demeanor, but he found himself on an emotional rollercoaster. One minute he was skeptical about the terrorist plot, and the next minute he was sure he was privy to a world-changing cataclysmic event. Finally, Sean worked up the courage to ask Chang, "How did your meeting with the Arab businessmen go?"

Chang eyed him suspiciously. "Camel jockeys looking for investors for another harebrained pipeline venture. Why do you ask?"

"No reason, really." Sean used an apathetic expression. It worked, Chang looked away indifferently.

That night, Sean boarded Chang's private jet for the flight back to New York. Chang apologized for not seeing his guest off saying that he had pressing business to attend to.

From the privacy of his office, Chang started making inquiries. His years as an arms dealer provided him with invaluable links to most of the major intelligence agencies. An agent working for the Soviet section of Great Britain's MI-6 confirmed a rumor about a missing atomic weapon from a Kazakhstan weapons cache. His special-ops contact at the KGB denied the gossip. Israeli's secret service, Mossad, couldn't corroborate what he'd already learned. After exhausting all of his sources, he was no closer to the unconditional truth he needed.

One way to validate the rumor was to contact a Chinese double agent imbedded in the Central Intelligence Agency. It would be dangerous because Chang would be violating his vow of confidentiality with the Arabs and he would be infringing on China's intelligence protocol.

That night, a forewarning came to Chang in a dream. He woke up and pushed the button on the ship's intercom barking, "I want to see the captain in my quarters immediately."

Chang was sitting behind his desk when the captain entered his stateroom. He drummed his fingers impatiently waiting for the sleepy-eyed man to come to attention. "Today, when you gave my American guest the tour, did you show him the communications room?"

The captain took two or three seconds to internalize the surprise question. Rather than answer he asked, "Is there a problem?"

"Listen to me carefully. Did you or my guest overhear anything that was said during my meeting with the Arab gentlemen?"

The captain's eyes darted anxiously. He answered drowsily. "I didn't hear anything. And besides, I don't speak Arabic."

"*Goeienaand*," Chang said rolling his good eye.

"Goodnight." The captain answered in English. He saluted and started to leave.

"Before you go, if you didn't overhear the conversation, how did you know they spoke Arabic?"

The captain shifted his weight nervously. "I...I reckon they spoke Arabic. They *were* dressed like Arabs, weren't they?" His improvising satisfied Chang. He dismissed him with a wave.

Chang went back to bed, but he couldn't sleep. He felt edgy, like he'd missed something. The same vision kept reappearing. He suppressed it, but was drawn back to it repeatedly. It was Robert Oppenheimer quoting Bhagavad Gita's scripture as he witnessed the first atomic explosion, 'Now I am become death, the destroyer of worlds.'

JAMES GARDNER

6

New York City

The Lincoln Town Car's tires made rhythmic thumps crossing the George Washington Bridge. Damn, I love this city, Sean thought. He looked at the darkened void where the World Trade Towers once stood and felt sick. He dialed the number of his producer, Harry Rosen and hung up. Immediately his cell phone chirped. Harry whispered groggily, "This better be the start of fuckin' World War Three."

"Harry, you have no idea how prophetic you've become. And no, it can't wait. I'll be there in fifteen minutes."

"What time is it?"

"A little after one," Sean said focusing on his wristwatch.

"You'll wake up the kids. Meet me at Elaine's."

Most of her Upper-Eastside customers had gone home. Two red-faced Irish-looking stockbrokers sat at the bar nursing Baileys. Elaine held court at her usual table in the back. Her audience was the regular collection of middle-aged desperate women. They stared at Sean as he sat down. Elaine gave him a nod. When she informed her friends about his shaky marital status, it piqued their interest. The women resumed their customary ranting about the lack of eligible men in the city.

Harry collapsed into the chair across from Sean. His comb-over made him look like he was undergoing chemo therapy. His clothes indicated colorblindness. "Like I said, kid, this better be fuckin earth-shattering." As he listened to Sean's eavesdropping recollection, his expression went from skepticism to curiosity and then reverted back to skepticism.

"Are you sure you overheard everything they said?" Harry yawned.

"I heard enough to scare me shitless."

"What's your read on Nelson Chang?"

"He's a genetic freak of nature. A genius many times over."

"Will he do the right thing?" Harry asked.

"If you mean, will he contact the CIA or the FBI. I'm doubtful."

"Hold that thought." Harry returned Elaine's glare. "We better order something before she has a conniption. Have you told anyone about this?"

"Not a living soul."

"Good. Sean, you're my best journalist, but let's look at the facts. What's the likelihood of you and those Arabs being on Chang's yacht at the same time? And then he provides you with the use of his private jet to keep you around for one more day. And you just happen to overhear this so-called secret meeting. To top it off, you're fluent in Arabic. Give me a break. We're missing something."

[40]

Sean used some time to digest Harry's unexpected compliment and then he asked, "So, what was Chang's motivation?"

Harry shook his head. He wiped the vestiges of sleep from his eyes. "As I see it, we've got two possible scenarios at work here. Either this is total horseshit, or I smell a Pulitzer."

"So, what do we do now?"

"We contact the CIA or Home Land Security or whoever."

"What happens to our project?"

"We shelve it."

Harry's limousine dropped Sean off in front of his Fifth Avenue apartment building. He took the elevator to the tenth floor. After undressing, he sank into an overstuffed recliner. He picked up a portrait of his wife sitting on the end table. It was the most beautiful face he'd ever seen. The familiar stomach-turning numbness returned. Rummaging through a stack of unpaid bills, he stopped when one caught his eye: $1500 for Jimmy Choo shoes. You've got to be kidding. She's got a closet filled with shoes.

He took a long hot shower. As he shaved, he looked at himself in the mirror. The hardened face that stared back was a stranger. He hadn't slept since leaving Hong Kong. Deep parenthesis outlined his mouth. Bags underlined bloodshot eyes. I need to find a new line of work before this one kills me, he thought. Sean was still too keyed-up to sleep. He let his burning eyes adjust to the dark. The radio clock seemed to be stuck on five. Wonder if Harry's in his office.

A guard motioned for Sean to bypass security. "Welcome home, Mr. Mahoney."

Harry Rosen's Guccis stuck out from underneath the *New York Times* entertainment section. "Well, I'll be damned—never expected to see you this early." Harry's hairpiece was tamed by a pair of tortoiseshell bifocals.

"I'm still on Hong Kong time."

"I reviewed the Chang interview. If you're having trouble sleeping, watch it."

"C'mon Harry, it can't be that bad."

"What did you and Chang do, fall in love and get married?"

"What did you expect? He laid down the rules."

"The suits upstairs have scheduled a meeting with an agent...," he stopped, searching for the name buried under some coffee-stained papers. "Here it is. Agent Robert Barrett, special agent with the CIA. His office at noon. We're to be accompanied by two in-house attorneys."

"Why do we need lawyers?"

"You need a lawyer when you take a crap in this country. You of all people should know about lawyers. For what it's worth, I think this thing's complete bullshit."

"Like I said before, you weren't there. I know what I heard."

Harry's telephone rang. Before he picked it up, he said, "You're right, kid, what the fuck do I know."

Sean scanned a week-old *Variety* while Harry talked on the telephone. Harry was right about the interview; it was weak. He wondered how Chang would react to Harry's edited version. He knew Harry wouldn't soft-pedal it. Chang will think he was betrayed by a man who he helped win fifty grand. At least be honest with yourself, it was a bribe. He remembered what Chang looked like. There were worse things than getting burned to a crisp, like going through a divorce.

"What time is it?" Sean asked Harry.

"8:30."

"I've got that meeting with the private detective. Later, Harry."

Harry held his hand over the receiver and whispered, "Make sure you're on time. The legal eagles need time to brief you."

JAMES GARDNER

7

Sean got out of a taxi at the corner of Lexington and West 33rd Street. Paddy's was a grungy little bar for serious drinkers. It smelled like the walls had been permeated by a hundred years of cigarette smoke and whiskey fumes. The motif consisted of black and white photographs of prizefighters. A life-size portrait of Paddy as a middleweight hung on the back wall. Paddy was pudgier now. His face looked like his time in the ring was spent as an Irish piñata. A grey-faced patron peeled a hardboiled egg. Another man read a racing form. A customer dozed with his head on the bar. Sean sat down in a booth in the back between the restrooms. There's always somebody to talk to in a bar like this one, he thought.

For the last six months his life had been a nightmare. He wasn't surprised when his wife asked him for a divorce. The disapproving looks—the turned cheeks when he tried to kiss her—the nightly excuses. He knew his marriage was shaky, but not unsalvageable. His wife disagreed. Ignoring Harry Rosen's advice, he hired a college fraternity brother as his lawyer who was outmatched by her lawyer, Morris Ackerman, known as "Moe the Megalodon." If the first arbitration had been a prizefight, the referee would have stopped it. If the fight had gone fifteen rounds, the judges would have scored it: 150 points for Manhattan College versus zippo for Yale.

At their latest deposition, Ackerman informed the Judge that his client was willing to settle for possession of their New York apartment and their home in East Hampton plus $50,000 a month in alimony. His wife's demands were so outrageous, Sean laughed.

He remembered his smile evaporating when the Judge asked, "What's so amusing, Mr. Mahoney?"

"But, Your Honor, she's asking for everything we own."

"The assets are jointly held. I find Mrs. Mahoney's requests quite reasonable. You've got thirty days to counter. Good day, sir."

The man who walked through the front door was wearing a Yankee baseball cap and a rumpled raincoat. Talk about straight out of central casting, Sean thought. His glasses were as thick as Coke bottles, which made him look bug-eyed. Acne had etched deep fissures in his cheeks. He needed a suntan.

The man whispered out of the side of his mouth. "You Mahoney?"

His teeth looked much too white not to be false, Sean figured. "That's me. What's your last name, Carmine?"

He ignored Sean. "Who gave you my name?"

[46]

"A mutual friend?"

"I don't have any friends. Did you bring the retainer? Hey, haven't I seen you on the idiot box?"

"I'm a television journalist." Sean slid an envelope across the table. "Think you can help me?"

Carmine clicked his fingers to get Paddy's attention and yelled, "Beer and a bump." He turned back to Sean. "That depends."

"On what?"

"I'll tell you that after you've answered some questions. Who's representing you?"

"Murphy. He's with Flaherty, Jones and McGraw."

"Never heard of him. And your wife's attorney?"

"Morris Ackerman."

"You're fucked and I mean big time."

"Thanks. They say you're a miracle worker."

Carmine glanced over both shoulders like he was afraid of eavesdroppers. "Who says?"

Sean shook his head and remained silent.

Carmine said, "Fair enough. I like a man who can keep his mouth shut. Did you bring the photograph of your wife like I asked you to?"

Sean handed him the picture. He held it up to the light and whistled seductively. "Wow, she's some piece of...," he stopped, catching himself. "Sorry 'bout that. She looks younger."

"Kathy's a former Miss Arkansas. You're right—she's younger than I am, twenty years to be exact."

"She looks familiar." Carmine eyed the photograph again. His puckered lips conveyed x-rated thoughts.

"Kathy's an international fashion model. She earns $5000 an hour."

[47]

"And now she wants to take you to the cleaners?" Carmine spit out the words like they were venomous. He wiped his lips. He leaned in masticating a wad of gum as rhythmically as a cow chewing its cud. His garlic breath caused Sean to recoil.

"Well, yes, I guess she does." Sean held his breath.

"Fuckin' women. They're all cunts. They can't help themselves: it's in their DNA. Mr. Mahoney, I'm gonna ask you a few simple questions. It's important that you give me straightforward answers. If you don't, you'll be wasting your money and my time. *Capishe*?"

The New Jersey in Carmine's voice was as irritating as fingernails scratching a chalkboard. Sean nodded that he understood.

"My first question's an easy one. Do you have any kids?"

"Kathy's my second wife. I have one daughter from a previous marriage."

Carmine stored the gum in his sagging jowl and asked, "So I take it, you've been through a divorce before?"

"My first wife died."

Carmine skipped the condolences. "Any kids with your present wife?" He sucked a gum bubble on the inside of his mouth and popped it. The sound added to Sean's irritation.

"No. Kathy never wanted children. She said childbirth would ruin her figure. She made me get a vasectomy after she got pregnant."

"I take it she had an abortion."

Sean nodded.

Paddy slid the whiskey and a beer chaser in front of Carmine. He guzzled the whiskey and slammed the shot-glass on the table. He shuddered as it hit bottom. "And I thought I just divorced the most self-centered bitch in history. My next question's important. Remember, I'm not a judge or a jury. Are you presently involved with another broad? Please be truthful."

"Absolutely not."

"Then it was your wife who asked for the divorce?"

"Yes."

"What reason did she give?"

"Irreconcilable differences."

"She's got someone porkin' her on the side," Carmine pronounced icily.

Sean leaned back, shaking his head. "That's impossible. Kathy's very religious." He looked traumatized.

Carmine rolled his eyes. He cracked his knuckles one at a time. "Friend, I don't give a shit if you're married to Mother Teresa. I've been doing domestic surveillance in this city for thirty friggin' years. And believe it or not, I've gone through six divorces myself. There's always a third side to these naughty triangles." He made quotation marks with his fingers around the word naughty. As he waited for Sean's answer, his pox-marked smirk expressed cynical amusement.

"You're wrong about this one."

"If I am, you've got my sincere apology. Just remember, divorces don't get settled in churches. Last question, do you love your wife?"

Sean's face reddened as he realized how dim-witted he sounded. He thought for a few long seconds, sighed and shook his head, but blurted, "Yes, in spite of everything, I still love her."

"Most men say they hate their estranged wives. Odds are, I'm gonna dig up some very nasty shit about your wife. You'll blame the messenger, all men do."

As Carmine waited for his words to sink in, he twirled a spoon between his fingers and then beat time with it on the table. Sean reached over and stopped him.

Sean thought, What makes you think I don't already hate you, but he said, "I'm desperate or I wouldn't be here."

"Exactly. In the past, some men have tried to stiff me. I wouldn't try it, if I were you. Female clients always pay, but men can be pricks, especially when their precious egos get stepped on.

"You won't have a problem with me or my ego."

"Good. Now that we understand each other, here's the way it goes down. If I get the goods on your wife, you pay me twenty-five big ones. I only take cash."

Sean felt his throat tighten. "What, no American Express?"

Sensing his annoyance, Carmine countered with, "Paying me twenty-five grand could be the best investment you've ever made."

"At this point, what have I got to lose, besides everything."

"I couldn't have put it better myself. She's a looker, which tilts the odds in our favor."

"You've only got three weeks," said Sean.

"That's a lifetime in my business. One more thing. Don't go near your wife. No phone calls. Nada. We need to give her space. Got it?" Carmine repositioned his dislodged dental plate with his tongue.

"Yup."

"I'll be in touch, Mr. Mahoney. Have a nice day. Oh, one small piece of advice. You can take it or leave it. Do yourself a favor—don't get hitched too soon."

"I'll never get married again."

"That's what all men say. Would you believe—I said it six friggin' times. Half my clients are repeat customers. Like I said, I'll be in touch. *Ciao.*"

As Sean watched Carmine leave, he felt the sudden urge to bathe.

8

The Central Intelligence Agency's regional office was relocated in a nondescript brownstone in Queens. The old address at 7 World Trade Center was destroyed by collateral damage on 9/11.

Sean, Harry and their lawyers presented themselves at the security desk. They emptied their pockets and opened their briefcases. One security guard checked their names off a list while another guard used a metal detecting wand. A well-dressed man approached them with some papers. After one of the lawyers scanned the papers, he said to Harry and Sean, "Sign on the dotted lines."

"What am I signing?" Harry asked. He wasn't wearing his toupee. He smoothed a few lonely strands of hair that had been blown out of place.

"Standard nondisclosure forms. This meeting's classified," stated the attorney. Harry made a wisecrack about the form protecting CIA from the media. The man presenting the form didn't see the humor.

"You're lawyers. There has to be a way to weasel out of this cloak and dagger horseshit," Harry said.

"Not a chance," said the other lawyer.

Agent Robert Barrett had a mop of white hair and a slight overbite. His pinstriped suit was cheap, but neatly pressed. Spit-shined wingtips indicated ex-military, Sean thought.

Barrett had worked for Blackwater Security before being recruited by the CIA. After the introductions and a contrived speech about the importance of patriotic Americans coming forward, Barrett motioned for everyone to be seated.

"Mr. Mahoney, why don't you tell me exactly what you overheard? Before you get started, I understand you speak Arabic."

"I majored in Middle Eastern studies at Yale."

"I'm impressed. I played fullback for Syracuse," Barrett said, trying to level the playing field.

"Now I'm the one impressed," Sean said.

"I wouldn't be. I fumbled twice in the Gator Bowl my senior year. Clemson kicked our ass. Why don't you start from the time you landed in Hong Kong."

One of the lawyers handed Barrett a copy of the contractual agreement between Nelson Chang and the network. After scanning the first page, he motioned for Sean to begin. Sean told him everything, excluding the money he won and his experience at Madam Fu's. Barrett listened with his hands supporting his chin, which highlighted his protruding teeth. As Sean repeated the conversation between the Arabs and Nelson Chang,

Barrett stopped him. "Stop right there! I have someone who needs to hear this firsthand."

Harry said, "Shouldn't you be taping this or at least taking notes?"

"You've been on camera since you exited your limo. Give us a little credit—we are in the intelligence-gathering business," Barrett said. Sean glanced at Harry and held his breath. Harry's expression divulged cynicism. Please don't mention the weapons of mass destruction, Sean thought.

Barrett excused himself.

He returned with a bearded Middle-Eastern-looking man.

"Mr. Mahoney, start at the point where you found yourself eavesdropping on the conversation between Mr. Chang and the Arabs. Please use Arabic."

After the interpreter and Sean conversed, the man told Barrett that Sean was indeed fluent. He complimented Sean on his command of Arabic and left the room.

Sean retold the eavesdropping incident in English. He thought for several moments and then concluded with, "I guess that just about covers everything."

"Mr. Mahoney, you've had one hell of an experience. If you have time, we've got some photographs I'd like to show you."

"Mug-shots?" asked Sean.

"That's right." Barrett replied, loosening his outdated tie.

Sean had done his duty. He felt relieved and it showed. "I'm happy to be of service."

"There's no need to remind each of you about the sensitive nature of this meeting. Everything we talked about this morning is strictly off the record. If we're all on the same page, you're free to go," said Barrett. Harry and Sean's thoughts were identical: Barrett made it sound like they were suspects in a criminal investigation.

"I need to get back to the studio," said Harry. "What about you two?" He asked the lawyers.

"No need for us to hang around."

Barrett had their lunch delivered in. Sean ate a tuna salad sandwich as he watched a slideshow of radical Islamists flashed on a large projection screen. Within one hour, he'd identified two of the Arabs and the Sudanese general. He asked Barrett some questions, but got no answers. As they parted company, Barrett thanked him and said that he would contact him in a few days.

A few days lapsed into ten. When Barrett didn't call, Harry said it was because Sean's eavesdropping epiphany was a nonevent. It was business as usual at the network. The edited version of the China documentary was electronically transmitted to Nelson Chang for his approval. Unexpectedly, the network received a temporary injunction prohibiting the airing of the segment citing the violation of Chang's right of editorial review. The network's lawyers and the law firm representing Nelson Chang tried to iron out the differences, but no progress was made.

Harry Rosen gave Sean a new assignment. Sean flew to Kentucky where he rented a car for the two-hour drive to Munfordville, a rural town seventy miles from Louisville. Harry had sent him to interview a country doctor about the nation's obesity pandemic for a segment entitled, "America's Health Crisis."

During the drive back to the Louisville Airport, Sean's mobile phone rang. "Mr. Mahoney, this is Robert Barrett. "I apologize for not getting back to you sooner. We needed time to corroborate your story."

"What does that mean?" Sean's hackles spiked.

"I didn't mean that the way it sounded."

"Well, how *did* you mean it?" Sean asked.

"The Arabs you overheard were trying to swindle Nelson Chang. We uncovered similar attempts to rip-off wealthy individuals. It's like one of those Nigerian chain letters. The one where they've got this great opportunity for you—all they need is seed money to get the ball rolling."

"You're positive this was a con job? I mean, three-hundred million is hardly seed money."

"Oh, there's no doubt about it." Barrett waited for a response. When he didn't get one, he added, "I assure you, we're on top of this."

"It's just that I remember you people telling the world about Iraq's buying that yellow cake in Niger. I'm sure you remember what started the war in Iraq."

"Not one of our finer moments. Once in awhile, we do get things right. Say, why don't you call me when you get back to New York? We can continue this discussion over lunch."

"You bet. I'll be in touch." Sean hung up. Screw you and the horse you rode in on. I'd rather have lunch with my wife's attorney, he thought.

Robert Barrett hung up and looked at his supervisor, who asked, "Well, did he buy it or not?"

"I think so. Poor guy's in for a rough time."

"Don't get schmaltzy on me. He won't be the only casualty."

"It isn't easy." Barrett said.

"It never is. Containing this is everything."

JAMES GARDNER

9

S ean returned Harry Rosen's call from the La Guardia airport terminal. "Why haven't you been answering your fuckin' phone?" Harry asked.

"'Cause, I've been traveling in a new invention—it's something called an airplane. What's up, doc?"

"Meet me at my apartment."

"What's wrong, Harry? You sound down in the dumps."

"Can't talk. Fill you in when I see you." Harry hung up.

Sean listened to the dial tone for a few seconds wondering what might be behind the call. He knew it wasn't good.

The doorman at Harry Rosen's building offered to store Sean's suitcase. Sean took the elevator to Harry's penthouse apartment. The front door was ajar.

"I'm in here," Harry yelled from his den.

"Where's Sara?" Sean asked.

"Shopping. I needed to talk to you in private. I fixed you your usual." Harry handed him a vodka martini. "Here's looking at you, kid." It was a poor Bogart imitation.

Sean took a sip and smacked his lips. "Did that guy, Barrett, call you?"

"Yup. I told you it was all bullshit. Harry's eyes said he was troubled. He eyed Sean closely for several seconds without saying a word.

"Why the long face, Harry? Well, say something, damn it."

Harry answered. "You better have a look at these." He flipped a large yellow manila envelope toward Sean who emptied it on the desk. There were glossy black and whites of him and the Chinese girls at Madam Fu's brothel engaged in every sexual combination imaginable.

Sean turned ashen. He fell onto the sofa and leaned back staring at the ceiling. He felt his heartbeat pounding in his ears.

"Are those the only copies?" He pointed at the photographs.

"I don't know. Look, I'm no saint. But we're the ones who are supposed to catch politicians doing this kinda perverted crap." He examined a photograph. "These girls look like they haven't reached puberty. Can you imagine what the tabloid pricks would do if they got their hands on these? I can almost see the headline, 'Pedophile, Sean Mahoney, caught in Asian love nest.' Why, they'd hang us by our balls."

Sean grimaced like he was holding his breath. "Have the suits upstairs seen them?"

"Sean, I didn't have a choice."

"Am I fired?"

"I believe the term they used was 'extended leave of absence.' At this point, I don't know why they didn't shit-can me."

"Why fire you?"

"Cost-cutting. My head's been on their chopping block for months. My guess is, they're only keeping me around long enough to clean up your mess."

Sean covered his face with his hands and mumbled, "How the hell am I supposed to earn a living? If my wife gets what she's asking for, I'll have to, as they say in Kentucky, 'take broke.'"

"If the press gets their paws on these, you're really screwed. You need some money, kid?"

"Nay, the attorneys would only get it."

"You can always write a tell-all book. That's what all defamed celebrities do. They write lousy books about how they screwed up their shitty lives."

"Thanks, Harry, I needed that. For the record, those girls are older than they look. Plus, I think they drugged me. In fact, I know they did."

"Well, isn't that wonderful fuckin' news? Hey, maybe this'll blow over. By the way, you need a better alibi than the old they-slipped-me-a-mickey defense. That one's a little overused."

The embarrassing silence ended with Sean blurting, "Don't you see—Chang's trying to ruin me. By discrediting me, he stops our segment. This is about what I overheard, despite what Barrett says."

Harry poured himself a refill and then handed the martini shaker to Sean. "I'll say one thing. You're a world class bull-shitter."

"What's that suppose to mean?"

"It means, and don't take this the wrong way, that you made up the eavesdropping episode to cover your ass in case someone found out about your little sex safari. Nobody, and I mean nobody, is gonna believe you."

"Not even you, Harry? You're my best friend."

"At this point, I'm your only friend. Okay, for argument's sake, let's say I don't believe you. In ten words or less —convince me."

"I swear on my daughter's life, I'm telling you the truth, the whole truth and nothing but the truth, so help me, God."

Harry took another swig of vodka. He swiveled his chair and looked down at a tugboat towing a gravel barge up the East River. Black smoke belched from the tug's smokestack. His trance was interrupted by an impatient horn-blower on the streets below. "You know something? I almost wish you *were* lying." Harry got up, walked over to the pool table in the middle of the room and racked the balls.

"What should I do—besides explain this to Kathy?"

"Are you kidding me? Your wife couldn't care less."

Sean looked unconvinced. "If I could just talk to her, I..."

Harry interrupted him. "Face it, kid, your marriage has been in the dumper for months."

Sean jumped up. "I gotta go!"

"Go where? The judge issued a restraining order against you."

"No, I mean I'm gonna be sick."

"Not on my silk Persians." Harry pointed and yelled, "The bathroom's that-a-way."

Sean ran to the bathroom. He felt nauseated and waited, but nothing happened. After a long moment it passed.

Sean's wounded look wasn't gone when he rejoined Harry. He leaned his head back and placed a damp washcloth over his face. "That bastard, Nelson Chang, ruined my life."

"You know what Mark Twain said, 'Foolish consistency is the hobgoblin of little minds.'"

"Emerson said it," said Sean.

"Whatever," acknowledged Harry. He lined up the cue ball and broke. "Your shot, kid."

Sean indicated that he wasn't in the mood to play. "By the way, Barrett never said the conversation didn't take place, He said those Arabs were trying to rip-off Chang."

Harry digested his comment as he tried a bank-shot. "You know something, you're absolutely right. One thing's for sure, we need to get you outta Gotham. And we need to hire a bodyguard. Someone to keep the paparazzi pricks at bay."

"What about Rigby Croxford?" Sean suggested.

Harry tried another bank-shot and missed again. "Doesn't your brother-in-law live in Africa? Isn't he in prison?"

"He was pardoned. Hey, don't look at me in that tone of voice. He was sent to prison on a trumped-up political charge."

"Can't you find someone a little closer, like maybe from Mars?"

"He's family. Don't worry, I'll get him here."

"You want some more bad news or the good news?" Harry put the pool cue aside and rubbed his hands together devilishly. A telltale grin seeped into his eyes.

"My life's such a cluster-fuck—I couldn't handle good news."

"The judge granted Kathy possession of your house in East Hampton. Your clothes and golf clubs are in my closet. She says you can live in the apartment until the divorce is finalized."

"My God, she's generous. How can it get any worse?" Sean shook his head.

Harry handed him a set of keys and some airline tickets. "The keys are to my Hatteras. She's docked in Key West. The ticket is to Miami. You'll need to rent a car at the airport."

"Isn't there another way?" Sean asked.

Harry hiked his shoulders. "You lay low. I'll take care of this end."

"I almost forgot. What was the good news?"

"Oh, that. My son was accepted at Trinity Prep." Harry put on a smile.

"Harry, you're such an asshole."

"Yes, but I have a great sense of comedic timing. Humor, my friend, is the essence of life."

"By the way, speaking of humor, you need to do something about your rug. People say you look like you've got a dead weasel sitting on your head."

"Who said that?" Harry spun around and looked at himself in the mirror behind his desk.

"Call you from Key West. Have a wonderful day."

Harry was too busy examining his hairpiece from different angles to say goodbye.

10

Nelson Chang's Gulfstream G-650 started a gradual descent from 40,000 feet. Chang had worked almost nonstop during the fourteen-hour transpacific flight from Hong Kong to an intersection two-hundred nautical miles west of the San Francisco International Airport. The floor around his seat was covered by crunched-up paper balls.

Chang didn't believe the jihadists' claim of having procured a nuclear device, but his curiosity got the best of him. The powerful intellect that had never failed him was being usurped by the onset of depression. Increasing his medication seemed to arrest the symptoms. Notwithstanding his apprehension, he was proceeding as if he believed they were telling the truth.

The economic disaster resulting from an atomic detonation in the United States would be world-changing. It was too risky not to take the preliminary steps to insulate China's burgeoning economy.

Chang envisioned two scenarios: The first one called for the liquidation of all assets with an American exposure. Those assets that couldn't be sold would be hedged. He would use credit-default-swaps to insure China's massive debt portfolio. The shorting of index futures would offset the funds' illiquid equity positions. Currency holdings would be arbitraged by buying gold and silver futures. China's sovereign funds' losses would be minimal.

The second strategy would only be implemented after he received absolute proof of the bomb's existence. The survival plan, as he inwardly referred to it, called for massive leverage by shorting index futures on all of the world's financial exchanges. The sovereign funds would buy option contracts on petroleum and precious metals as well as other strategic minerals. By Chang's calculations, this strategy had the potential of making enormous profits.

Chang had not confided in anyone about the plot, nor did he intend to, at least for the time being. If this was a hoax, he might be seen as naïve. A man managing four trillion dollars couldn't afford to be seen as gullible.

Ho Leng worked as a research analyst for the Far East Division of the Central Intelligence Agency in McClain, Virginia. She was a graduate of both the Massachusetts Institute of Technology and Columbia. It had taken Chinese operatives two years to recruit Leng. She had an insatiable appetite for everything her government salary couldn't afford. Leng's expertise was industrial espionage. As a double agent, her primary role was to keep Chang apprised of technological innovations that could affect China's economy. The intelligence she passed to Chang was so mundane she couldn't believe anyone was dumb enough to pay her for data that was for the most part, listed in the public record. That was about to change.

Chang chose San Francisco's Chinatown for his meeting with Ho Leng. Like Chang, she also spoke fluent German. Their presence wouldn't attract attention, and nosey eavesdroppers wouldn't be a problem.

Chang studied Leng from the backseat of a limousine as she entered the restaurant. He waited to make sure she wasn't being followed.

Leng watched Chang enter the restaurant. He wore sunglasses and a hat, but it wasn't enough to hide his deformities. She moved uneasily as he sat down.

"Permit me to introduce myself." Chang used perfect German.

"I know who you are," Leng said shaking his hand.

"I'm the one who's been sending you the extra money. I thought it was time we met. I need the information I requested for reasons that shouldn't concern you. I will say this—you and I are linked by the same patriotic principles."

Leng pushed back, took a deep breath and ran her fingers through her raven-black hair. "You can save the civics lesson. What about the money?"

"It's all in here." He pushed a briefcase underneath the table. "Now, what were you able to find out?"

"Your intel is spot-on. A weapon was stolen from a Russian battery. It seems two Russian generals..." Chang stopped her by raising his hand as a Chinese couple walked past them and sat down at the lunch counter. Chang was surprised by her comment. Despite acting nonchalant, she noted the change. Lost in thought, he closed his good eye before giving her the nod to continue.

"It was sold by the two Russian generals, but never delivered," she whispered.

"You're positive the weapon's still on Russia soil?" Chang thought the Russians would never admit to losing control of a nuclear weapon. "I'm not sure I'm buying that last part."

"Which part?" Leng asked.

"I have no doubt the generals sold the weapon. The KGB would never admit to such incompetence. The weapon might still be in Russia or anywhere else for that matter."

"The agency's official position is that the Russians have control of the situation." Leng restated. "The KGB is out of my sphere."

Chang chose his next words carefully. "A miniaturized device is easy to hide." He waited for her clarification.

"It wasn't a suitcase variety. It was a uranium-235 fission mega-bomb."

He cleared his throat. "How many kilotons are we talking about?"

"Twenty," she replied. "Like I said, my source says the KGB has secured the weapon. Really, it's no longer a problem."

Chang's expression gave no indication of his thinking, but she guessed he was corroborating what he already knew.

"What transpired at the meeting between the television reporter, Sean Mahoney, and your agent in New York City?"

"The agency believes you were the target of a sophisticated swindle attempt. That's everything I know. If you're done with me, I'd like to go." She fidgeted nervously waiting for his permission to leave.

He turned off the tape recorder hidden in his pocket. If the terrorist attack was authentic, he now had proof that he had warned the CIA. Ho Leng would be exposed, but that wasn't his concern. Besides, she's a money-grubbing unprincipled bitch.

He placed his gloved hand on her forearm and squeezed so hard she winced. His voice became harsh. "If you discuss what we talked about with anyone, I promise you that your time on this planet will be very limited. Rest assured —this is not an idle threat. Do we understand each other, Ms. Leng?"

His cruelty made her gasp. She nodded that she understood.

"*Auf wiedereshen.*" Without looking up, he snapped his fingers in a bug-off gesture.

She fought back tears and rubbed her forearm.

Ho Leng exited the restaurant and ran to catch a cable car. Two men approached her from behind and hooked her elbows. One of them whispered in her ear, "Someone we know is very anxious to hear what your friend, Mr. Chang, had to say. Here, let me help you with that." The man whispering grabbed her briefcase. They whisked her between two parked cars and into a black Ford Explorer with darkened windows.

JAMES GARDNER

11

The eighteen-hour flight from Johannesburg to New York was behind schedule. Bloody airline seats were designed for midgets, Rigby Croxford thought, stretching to relieve the numbness in his legs. He was awake now and sweaty. Something had triggered one of his reoccurring nightmares about his time in Hwange prison. But the really bad ones were about his years in the Rhodesian War and were his nightly companions.

He thought about his wife and smiled inwardly. In spite of the hardships, Helen loves living in Africa more than I do, he thought. Mercifully, the droning jet engines lulled him into submission. He fell asleep recalling the conversation that was the reason for this trip.

"We need to talk," she said. Her eyes indicated trouble.

"I'm all ears, my love." I fortified myself with more brandy.

"Here, read this." She tried to hand me a letter.

"Tell me what it says."

"It's from Sean. He's had a few setbacks."

"Oh, what kind of setbacks?"

"He's been fired and his wife left him and something else has happened. To top it off, he's drinking to excess again. He says he'll fill you in on the details when you get there."

"First of all, you don't even like your brother's wife. Secondly, I drink to excess. Look what it's done for me."

She frowned saying, "I wouldn't go there if I were you."

"And what on earth do you mean, when I get there?" I said.

"I never said I didn't like his wife. I said I thought she was too young for Sean. He sent you these." She handed me airline tickets.

"Sean needs your help or he wouldn't ask."

"What the hell can I do?"

She placed her hand over my glass. "I guess you'll just have to fly to the States and find out."

I couldn't give in without a little pushback. She was always so damned appealing when she was pissed off. "He's your brother." This will get her goat. I lit another cigarette and exhaled smoke at her.

She protested by paddling the air. "He doesn't want me —he wants you."

"How about you coming with me?"

"This isn't a good time for me," she said

"It sounds like this isn't a bloody good time for your brother."

"That's not fair and you know it. I've got my patients to look after. And there's my politics."

"You're impossible. When do I leave?"

"In three days. You end up in Key West by way of New York and Miami. Look at the bright side —you get to spend time with Jesse Spooner." She grabbed my cigarette and flicked it over the railing. *"You promised to quit smoking."*

"I was about to quit, but this trip's upset me."

"You're impossible," she said.

Rigby Croxford was still reminiscing when the Boeing-747 touched down in New York at dusk.

He missed his connecting flight to Miami. After booking the next available flight, he took a bus to the midtown terminal in Manhattan.

To kill time, he walked the streets. People moved at and around him without making eye contact. The hustle and bustle caused a sensory overload. He bought a soft pretzel from a street vendor and sat down on a park bench facing Fifth Avenue. From time to time people sat down next to him. When he tried to engage them, they got up and walked away. The last person who sat down was an old black man pushing a shopping cart. His thread-bare overcoat was large enough for a man twice his size. He wore three sweaters under his coat, a woolen ski-cap and sunglasses. Sciatica had bent him into a question mark.

"Nice day. I'm Rigby Croxford." He extended his hand.

"Smells like rain to me. Gladstone's the name." The old man removed the ski-cap and smoothed out his corn-rows.

"What's so bad about rain?" Rigby asked.

"Nothin', if you live under a roof. I sleep in the park."

"Are you in the can business?" Rigby noted the man's shopping cart was filled with empty aluminum cans. The bottom rack contained his life's belongings.

"No, I'm president of the New York Stock Exchange. Say, friend, how about we have us a little snort?" He removed a bottle wrapped in a brown paper bag from his coat pocket. After scanning the area, he handed the bottle to Rigby.

"You like living outdoors?"

Gladstone retrieved cigarette butts from his coat pocket until he found one that he liked. "Its seventh heaven, if you don't mind dog shit." His nose wrinkled. "Lately, I've been thinkin' about spendin' my winters in Palm Beach. Know what I mean?"

Rigby laughed. "You made my day." He lit the man's stub and then his own cigarette.

"Say friend, I'm gonna take me a little snooze. How about keepin' an eye out for me?"

"Who am I looking for?" Rigby asked.

"It ain't naked ladies. The pigs, that's who. A flatfoot named Mulligan in particular."

The old man dozed off while Rigby stood watch. The barnyard smell of the horse-drawn carriages reminded him of Africa. A cool breeze loosened the few remaining leaves and sent them fluttering to the ground. The leafless limbs looked like boney arthritic hands protesting winter. Rigby's head bobbed a few times and then he fell asleep.

An hour later, he was awakened by a policeman jabbing him in the ribs with a nightstick.

"Gladstone, how many times have I told you not to sleep on these benches? Jesus, don't you ever learn. Now, take your friend and find a shelter," the cop said, shining a flashlight in their faces. Mulligan grabbed Gladstone's bottle and poured the contents in the gutter. Gladstone groaned like he'd been gut shot.

"An Irishman wasting good whiskey is a mortal sin."

Rigby squinted. "I didn't know sleeping was against the law in this country."

"Oh, so you're the comedian in this act. Get movin' or you'll both be sleepin' it off behind bars."

The old man shook hands with Rigby and said goodbye. Rigby slung his duffel bag over his shoulder and walked away. Twice, he glanced back at the policeman who continued to watch him. Two blocks later, he waved goodbye and crossed Fifth Avenue.

Rigby entered a small hotel lobby. The well-dressed man behind receptionist desk visually raked him from head to toe. Peering over bifocals wrinkled the man's nose.

"Can I help you, sir?" His voice was contaminated by a lisp.

Rigby noted the surrounding opulence. "I'd like a room."

"Oookay," the man answered leisurely. He slid a registration card and a pen across the counter. "What a lovely accent. You must be English."

"I'm Rhodesian, actually. Before I fill this out, how much do you charge for a room?"

"That's 450."

"Good, God, I need it for one night, not a bloody month."

"Let me guess. I bet this is your first visit to the Big Apple."

"I just arrived from Zimbabwe. I missed my connection to Miami."

"Honey, the 450 is for one night. Welcome to New York City."

"Ouch! I think I'll bed-down over in the park."

The clerk clasped his face theatrically. "Dear God in heaven, you'll get mugged for sure. There are robbers running amuck in Central Park after dark."

Rigby noticed the man's polished fingernails. He shoved his hands in his pockets to hide them. "I've got news for you —there are robbers running the hotels in this city."

The desk clerk pouted. "I don't set the rates. I only work here. Well, how much can you afford?" He looked very annoyed. He supported his chin with both fists waiting for Rigby's answer.

"I could go maybe a hundred at best."

"You can't rent a room in a bedbug and beyond for a hundred bucks in this city. My advice is to wait for your flight at the airport."

"You bet. Sorry about the misunderstanding."

"Don't worry about it. You take care." He batted his eyes.

Jamal and Lavon watched Rigby leave the hotel. Their customized low-rider was a white Coup Deville. The Cadillac had illuminated spinning hubcaps on oversized tires. Tinted windows pulsated from booming rap music.

Lavon muted the radio. "Whatdayathink?"

"I'd say the dude has money or he wouldn't be stayin' at that fancy hotel."

"I think we done got ourselves one. Drive around the block."

When they circled back around they found Rigby trying to hail a taxi.

Jamal yelled, "Hey mister, you lookin' for a lift?"

Rigby stepped from the curb. "I could sure use a ride to the airport."

"Kennedy or La Guardia?"

"La Guardia."

"How does thirty fish sound?"

"If you mean dollars, you got yourself a deal." Rigby climbed into the backseat.

The driver's shaved head shined like an eight-ball. The man riding shotgun wore his hair in dreadlocks. He looked like he was wearing a dead tarantula for a hat. The car reeked of sweet cologne.

Instead of crossing the East River, the driver skirted Central Park and headed straight for Harlem. Rigby tried to strike up a conversation, but they ignored him. Lavon turned down a deserted street lined by darkened tenements. Rigby noticed men standing around a fire-barrel warming their hands. The neighborhood had a rundown desperate feel. They parked at the end of the street. Jamal and Lavon's cigarettes provided the only light.

"This doesn't look like the airport," Rigby said.

"No shit, Sherlock. You see, me and Lavon ain't really in the taxi business. We're in the takin' care of business, business. Ain't that right, Lavon?"

Rigby paused and then he said calmly, "If you two gentlemen are thinking about robbing me, I think you should reconsider your options."

"Listen to the man. He says we should reconsider our options." They both laughed.

"Hey, dude, do yourself a favor. Just give us your money and walk away." Jamal pulled a large knife from under his seat. He tilted the blade letting it glitter in the dull light. "You don't want me cuttin' you up. Tell him, Lavon."

"No fuckin' way. Hell no. Jamal's good with a knife."

Rigby sighed dejectedly. He shrugged and dropped his wallet on the front seat. As Jamal reached for it, Rigby used the distraction to deliver a bone-crushing elbow to Jamal's temple. His head produced a spiraling crack in the side window. Rigby ended up holding the knife. Only the seatbelt prevented the man's body from slumping forward.

Lavon screamed, "You crazy motherfucker, you kilt him."

"I didn't kill anyone. Now, drive me to the airport."

Jamal gurgled incoherently. Lavon mumbled, "What's you gonna do to us?"

"I haven't decided about that, yet. Keep your eyes on the road."

Jamal started to regain consciousness just as they pulled up in front of the terminal.

"Stop right here." Rigby handed Lavon thirty dollars. "Sorry about your mate." Rigby lobbed Jamal's knife into a trash can and disappeared into a revolving door.

Jamal blinked his eyes and came to. "Damn, bro, what the fuck did you hit?" He rubbed his temples. "What happened to the cracker? Did we get his money?"

"The white dude sucker-punched you."

"Say what?" Jamal asked rolling his neck. He jiggled his jaw and winced.

"Bro, he knocked you out."

"That honky's lucky he hauled ass. 'Cause I would've gone upside his mother-fuckin head. That's all I'm sayin'." Jamal shook out the cobwebs. "I should've cut him."

Lavon said, "I don't know, bro. That dude was tough."

"Shit. I would've kicked his white ass sideways. You hear what I'm sayin'?"

Lavon's giggling was met by Jamal asking, "What's so fuckin' funny?"

Lavon pinched his nose and asked nasally, "Did you just shit? What kinda food you been eatin' boy?"

Jamal also sniffed. "God damn it, I just bought these threads."

Lavon pleaded. "C'mon, man, give me a break—roll down the fuckin' window."

JAMES GARDNER

12

Miami

There was never a more unlikely friendship. Jesse Spooner, the black ATF agent, and Rigby Croxford, a white Rhodesian farmer, had a shaky beginning. They met under harrowing circumstances. Surviving an African insurrection bonded them for life.

As an ATF agent, Jesse had recently been reassigned to the Port of Miami where he inspected cargo containers shipped from Central and South America. His department was so understaffed, Jesse said the odds of intercepting illegal contraband were about the same as winning the Florida lottery.

When Jesse met Rigby at the Miami International Airport, Rigby tried to shake hands, but Jesse smothered him in a bear hug. "God damn, can't believe you finally made it. How's the better half?"

"Helen's well. She sends you her best."

"So, how was New York City?" Jesse grabbed Rigby's duffel bag.

"Bloody expensive."

"What brings you to Miami?"

"Buy me a beer and I'll fill you in."

"I have some vacation time coming. Tomorrow, I'm taking you fishing. There's a tournament going on. I hired the best fishing guide in the Keys. With a little luck we might win the whole enchilada."

"Hold on, Jesse. I'm here to sort out my brother-in-law's problem or problems, whatever the case might be. After that, I'm all yours."

Jesse couldn't hide his disappointment. "Well, shit, I was looking forward to this. Must be important."

Rigby told Jesse what he knew about his brother-in-law's situation, but mostly they reminisced about their time together in Africa. Jesse tried to convince Rigby to spend the night, but he was antsy to get on the road. After he promised to spend time in Miami before flying back to Zimbabwe, they parted company.

Rigby headed south in a rental car. The Overseas Highway connects Miami to Key West. The windless day made the ocean oily smooth. Occasionally, brown-pelican formations interrupted the monotonous horizon. The sun dropping into the Gulf of Mexico painted the sunset with strokes of crimson and yellow. The shorelines bordering the highway were punctuated by droopy palm trees and Australian pines. The promise of night accented the air with night-blooming jasmine. As Rigby crossed the last bridge marking the city limits, he thought about Jesse's saying that Key West can mark a man's soul with unseen graffiti. He described Key West's inhabitants as a blend of artsy types and locals mixed in with a few Jimmy Buffet wannabes. I'm gonna like this town, he thought.

After searching for an hour, he gave up and asked directions from a man sitting in a rocking chair on a porch. His shack was partially hidden by slatted stone-crab traps and fishing nets. The man's face bore damage from sea-work. A cigarette sent smoke into his eyes.

The old man squinted and cocked back his baseball cap. "Kin I hep ya?"

"I'm lost. Which way is Key West?"

"Tother end of the island, friend. This is Stock Island. Not that freak show." The man recocked his cap. "You head towards the settin' sun. You'll find it." He rubbed blood back into his barnacled fingers and resumed the net mending.

"Sorry to bother you," Rigby shouted.

The old man yelled back without looking up. "Wasn't no trouble."

The light was failing by the time Rigby entered the marina's parking lot. A night watchman pointed at Harry Rosen's Hatteras. The Second Take lay captive to her moorings at the end of a pier. She was a fifty-foot Hatteras in need of some spit and polish.

Rigby knocked on the pilothouse bulkhead. The cabin's curtains were drawn so tight only threads of light escaped. He was about to walk back to the dock-master's office when he saw someone peeking out from behind a cracked door.

"Rigby, is that you?" Sean yelled.

"At your service," Rigby shouted back.

As soon as Rigby entered the cabin, Sean latched the door behind him. A cocktail table was cluttered with dirty glasses and a smelly pizza box. When they shook hands,

Sean held Rigby's longer than necessary. He was unshaven and his eyes were bloodshot.

"Sean, is everything alright?"

"I'm okay, considering."

"I didn't know you smoked." Rigby noted an overflowing ashtray.

"Right about now, lung cancer is the least of my worries. Can I offer you a drink?"

"A whiskey would be lovely."

"One whiskey, coming up. Make yourself comfortable. Christ, it's good to see you. How long's it been?" He answered his own question. "Must be ten years. How's my sister?"

"She's well." Rigby picked up a pizza slice that hung so unappetizingly limp, he rejected it. He sniffed his fingers and then rubbed them on his pants.

Sean yelled up from the galley. "Helen must be elated about my getting a divorce. She never liked Kathy."

"Your sister only wants you to be happy." Rigby squashed his cigarette butt in the pizza box and lit another one.

"If my soon-to-be ex-wife gets her way, I'll be an unemployed beggar. Here's mud in your eye." He hoisted his glass and clicked it against Rigby's. "I can't tell you how much I appreciate your coming over."

Rigby raised his glass and toasted with, "Cheers."

It took Sean the better part of an hour to chronicle the events that had turned his life upside down. He started with his Hong Kong assignment and the interview with Nelson Chang. His description of Chang's meeting with the Arabs piqued Rigby's curiosity, but when Sean described his meeting with the Central Intelligence Agency characterizing what he overheard as an attempted swindle, he seemed to lose interest. Sean didn't omit his experience at Madam Fu's or the fifty-thousand dollars he won, which he described as a bribe. He ended by telling him about the photographs being sent to the network and his subsequent firing.

"I must say, old boy, you have been through a rather rough spell," said Rigby. As an African, the China-Chang connection interests me. If you remember, a few years ago, your sister and I ended up in the middle of a Sudanese uprising, for want of a better term. I found out that Nelson Chang was the arms dealer selling weapons to the Arab militias in the Sudan. Some people say the killing of indigenous Africans was indirectly financed by the Chinese government. Seems they wanted access to oil reserves in the Darfur. I won't bore you with the details, but suffice it to say, Khartoum has been at the center of terrorism on the African continent. One thing's for sure, China and the Sudanese government are joined at the hip. Anyway, Chang was severely burned in a helicopter crash in the Sudan. At the time, we all thought he was killed. It seems our Mr. Chang has nine lives."

"When I interviewed Chang, I confronted him with those same accusations. He denied any connection between his government and the atrocities in the Sudan."

"Take it from someone who lives there, China's a key player in Africa, and for all of the wrong reasons." Rigby cleared his throat, mostly to himself, and grumbled, "I should've made a more concerted effort to kill the bastard when I had the chance. Bloody bad luck, actually."

His violent expression shocked Sean, but Rigby was too lost in his thoughts to notice.

Sean said, "I've been a reporter for twenty-something years, which means I've interviewed some very accomplished liars, like American politicians, for instance. I believe those Arabs were telling Nelson Chang the truth. For some reason, this guy Barrett's trying to sweep this thing under the rug."

Rigby held up his empty glass requesting a refill. "Be that as it may, what's Barrett's motivation?"

"To tell you the truth, I haven't a clue. Look at the facts. Why would those Arabs try to swindle Chang? The man's a genius, albeit an evil one. Christ, he speaks better Arabic than they do. There must be easier victims to con."

Rigby said, "Most Arabs are still in the Dark Ages. Plus, you said Chang has access to big Chinese money."

"It still doesn't add up." Sean rubbed his chin stubble waiting for his brother-in-law's response. "Well, whatdaya think?"

"I think you've been watching too many James Bond movies."

"Now, you sound like my producer. I know this sounds even crazier. I've seen two men watching this boat."

Deep in thought, Rigby drew heavily on a cigarette. He spoke through the exhaled smoke. "Probably secret agents?" His grin melted into a frown and then reverted back to a smile.

"I must sound crazy," Sean said.

"A little. What's the status of your documentary?"

"Everything's on hold. My network's waiting to see if my laundry gets aired. I can't blame them much."

"And you feel that's why Chang got you fired?"

"Chang doesn't need to be in the limelight. Not if this Arab thing's for real. Don't you see, by discrediting me, everything at the network comes to a standstill."

They were silent as Rigby digested Sean's guesswork. He drained the last drop of whiskey from his glass and muttered, "Tomorrow we'll make a plan. Right now, I can hardly keep my eyes open."

"So, you don't think I'm insane?"

"Ask me tomorrow."

13

Rigby Croxford attributed his nightmares to the trials and tribulations of living in Africa. Mentioning the Sudanese insurrection elicited an old favorite. He fell asleep reliving the charge of screaming Arabs wearing black flowing robes riding decorated war camels and horses. He heard the crack and whistle of gunfire and the thumps of sullied human flesh. The desert was littered with corpses, grotesque and horrifying. The noise of whirling rotor-blades overwhelmed the screams of dying men and death-bellowing animals. His nightmare ended with a vision of Chang's helicopter spinning out of control and the ensuing orange explosion.

The persistent urge to urinate woke him up. Dulled from sleep, Rigby slipped out of his bunk. Screeching seagulls brought him back to the present. I'm on boat in Key West, he thought. He turned on the cabin light, reached for his cigarettes and found the following note:

Dear Sleeping Beauty,

Thought I'd better let you sleep in.
Gone shopping.
Coffee is on the stove.
Back in two hours.

Sean

Rigby smoked his first cigarette of the day on the Second Take's stern. The marina was busy. Blue runners chased minnows to the surface where seagulls plucked them up. Giant silver-sided tarpon rolled beneath fish-cleaning stations anticipating fish scraps. Pelicans begged for leftovers. Boat captains worked the tourists trying to sell fishing charters.

Rigby noticed someone taking photographs of him from a parked car. Curiosity got the best of him. He walked down the dock and circled back around from the other end of the marina. When he knocked on the car window, the man with the camera ignored him. He banged harder. This time, the man rolled down the window.

"Gotta a match?" Rigby asked improvising.

The man ignored him and closed the window. Rigby knocked harder this time. Before he could speak, the man shouted, "Get away from the car, asshole."

When Rigby refused to move, the man barked, "Are you fuckin' deaf? I said, get lost."

Rigby felt his pulse rate quicken. Blood reddened his face to the color of Warhol's soup can.

What is it about this country? That's the second time this week someone's threatened me, he thought.

"Look, you limey creep... " The man never finished the sentence. Rigby reached in, grabbed him by the collar and jerked his head out through the half-opened window. The glass skinned the man's nose like a potato peeler. Rigby braced his foot against the door and heaved until the man's head popped out.

"I can accept rude behavior, but no one calls me a limey."

"I can't breathe." The driver clutched at his throat.

Rigby never saw the man riding shotgun get out. He felt something dig deep in his ribs. He heard. "I should cut your spine in two. Now, back off nice and easy, asshole."

Rigby raised his hands. After extricating his friend's head, the passenger jumped into the driver's seat and shouted, "I don't know who the hell you are, but I hope we meet again real soon."

"It'll be my distinct pleasure, old chap." Rigby saluted and flashed a smile.

The man was so incensed, he gunned it and almost slammed into a parked car.

Sean knew something was wrong when he saw two police cars parked behind Harry's Hatteras.

"Care to tell me, what the hell's going on?" said Sean.

After listening to Rigby, Sean said, "So, I'm not so crazy, after all. Wonder who they work for?"

The doubt was still in Rigby's eyes, but it was less evident now. "I better call Jesse Spooner."

"Doesn't Spooner work for the government?"

"That's right," replied Rigby.

"You trust him?"

"Spooner? I trust him more than any man I've ever known. With the exception of you, of course," Rigby hastened to add.

Sean knew this wasn't true. He'd heard too many stories about Jesse Spooner.

*　　*　　*

Jesse Spooner stood on the bow of a flats-boat in Biscayne Bay. The fishing guide standing on the poling platform used a push-pole to stem the current. A sandbar blocked the entrance to a lagoon bordered by tangled mangroves. Their quarry was a school of bonefish. Jesse had already landed a tarpon and a permit. A bonefish would complete the grand slam. Any fish in the school would win the Upper Keys Grand Tournament. First prize was Gold Rolex watches for the angler and the guide.

"Hang in there. Tide's rising. Another five minutes — you'll get your shot," the guide whispered and then added as a warning, "Make a sound, you'll spook 'em."

Jesse used his hand to block the sun's glare. He rechecked the fly-line coiled at his feet. The fly-rod suddenly felt unwieldy. He adjusted the length of fly-tippet dangling in the gin-clear water. He felt the boat move as the guide heaved on his pole.

The tailing bonefish had been feeding on blue crabs in the lagoon's turtle grass. The fear of getting stranded by a falling tide would make them move. Their exposed sickle tails glistened in the sunlight. In seconds the fish would be within Jesse's casting ability. Grey silt puffs boiled behind the feeding fish.

"Two o'clock—forty feet," the guide whispered. He squatted to prevent his shadow.

Jesse dared a look. His heart rate increased. The lead fish was now close enough. He was making the third false cast when his cell-phone chimed. He grabbed for the phone with the urgency of someone who had one go off at a funeral. He fumbled with the phone and dropped his car keys in the process. The sound of the keys hitting the deck was deafening in the stillness. Bonefish exploded in every direction. The guide screamed obscenities.

"Croxford, this better be important," Jesse whispered. He shrugged apologetically at the fishing guide who threw his arms up.

"I wouldn't be calling if it wasn't. I need you here, now."

"Mind telling me, why?" he asked Rigby.

"I got myself in a bit of a pinch."

"Croxford, the last time you used those words, you damn near got me killed."

"Why do you always look at the negative side? Enough chit-chat—get your ass in gear."

"Keep the lights burning. I'm on my way."

Six hours later, Jesse arrived in Key West. After introductions, Rigby asked Sean to recount his story. When Sean mentioned Chang, Jesse interrupted him. "I know more about Nelson Chang than I care to. A few years back, I was sent to Africa to investigate his arms trafficking. I ended up in the middle of a civil war. Your-brother-in-law saved my ass." He noted Rigby. He checked the time on his Timex, then held it to his ear and sighed.

"I reckon we saved each other's asses," said Rigby.

Jesse continued. "Anyway, we both thought Chang was killed in a helicopter crash. Then, out of the blue, I hear he's been resurrected. When I saw the crash," He looked at Rigby for confirmation, "I remember thinking—no one survives that. Makes you wonder if a man ever really gets his just rewards."

"Chang lost an eye and his burns are hideous," Sean said.

Jesse shook his head. "Hard feeling sympathy for Chang. He's responsible for a lot of suffering in this world."

Sean said, "One thing's for sure, he doesn't feel one iota of guilt. And if what I overheard Chang and those Arabs planning is real, his past sins will pale by comparison."

Sean's dire prophesy quieted them.

Normally, Jesse would recommend contacting the Central Intelligence Agency, but Sean had already told him, "been there, tried that." He considered mentioning Gordon Wells. Gordon had retired from the CIA, and he lived in Key West. For the time being, he decided to postpone telling them about his friend.

Later that night, at a local bar, Sean asked, "So, Jesse, what really happened in Africa?"

"You mean, besides your brother-in-law almost getting me killed?"

"You're embellishing again," Rigby said.

"The hell I am," Jesse slurred.

"You never let the facts get in the way of a good story." Rigby smiled indulgently.

Sean appeared dumbstruck. "My sister was right about you two. You're both completely insane." His chirping cell phone prevented the next question. He excused himself and stepped away from the table. He cradled the phone and apologized by throwing up his hands. It was his lawyer requesting more details about his upcoming property settlement. Sean hung up and sighed. He looked dejected. Rigby got the waiter's attention and ordered more drinks.

The celebration lasted into the wee hours. A few locals gathered at the bar to hear Rigby's stories. No man was a better raconteur.

"Quiet, please. The floor is yours, sir," Jesse said to Rigby.

He stood up, cleared his throat and recited the following:

> *Half a league, half a league, half a league onward.*
> *All in the valley of Death rode the six hundred.*
> *"Forward, the Light Brigade!"*
> *Charge for the guns! he said.*
> *Into the valley of valley of Death rode the six hundred.*
> *Et cetera, et cetera, et cetera.*

"What about the rest of it?" Jesse asked.

"I'm too sloshed, my friend. And with that, Lord Tennyson and I wish you all a fond farewell."

*   *   *

The next morning, Jesse pressed his temples and groaned. "Someone's at the door."

"I must say, old boy, I do believe the knocking's in your head. Sean, you look rather chipper this morning," Rigby said.

"I feel like my head's in a trashcan and someone's beating it with a hammer. You two look like death warmed over."

"Enough compliments. Rest assured we feel worse than we look. What's on today's agenda?" Rigby belched painfully.

Jesse held his Timex to his ear and then thumped it with his knuckle. "I've arranged a meeting with an old friend. Gordon Wells worked for the CIA for twenty years."

Noting Sean's questioning look, Jesse added, "I know it's a long-shot. You know what they say, 'nothing ventured, nothing gained.'"

When Jesse mentioned Gordon Wells, he explained that there was a possibility that Gordon might be reluctant about helping them considering the circumstances surrounding his separation from the CIA. He decided to let Gordon fill them in on the details.

14

Most of the houses in Key West are painted in pastels and are trimmed with fancy wooden lattices. The few neglected ones have been sandblasted by hurricanes and standout like pimples on a beautiful girl's face. Gordon Wells's picturesque cottage was framed by purple bougainvillea vines and white oleander bushes. The redbrick walkway was lined with pink impatiens.

At five o'clock on the dot, Jesse knocked on the front door. The woman who opened the door introduced herself as Laura, Gordon Wells's daughter. Her sun-streaked auburn hair was secured in a ponytail. Emerald green eyes and freckles highlighted an honest-looking face. Her teeth were crooked in a way that made them sexy. She wore Levis and a pink button-down shirt knotted at the waist. She hugged Jesse and shook hands with Sean and Rigby.

"He's been waiting all day and making me miserable." She spoke with a slight southern twang. "He's out back with his orchids." Her tone took on a teasing quality. "I must say, ya'll look a little piqued. Can I offer you sundowners?"

"Yes, ma'am," Sean answered. Rigby nodded enthusiastically.

They followed Jesse though the house. Stuffed bookshelves and tropical plants made it cozy. The backdoor opened onto a ramp connected to a glass vaulted greenhouse.

The temperature inside was suffocating. Even so, Gordon Wells wore a white smock. He was hunched over a microscope. A transparent fluid bag hung from a rack attached to the back of his wheelchair. An intravenous drip tube disappeared into the back of his hand. Oblivious to their presence, he conducted a recording of Mozart's Third Horn Concerto. Gordon Wells was dreadfully thin. His eyes didn't match his weakened condition.

"Well, well, if it isn't the great Jesse Spooner. What took you so long? Hello, I'm what's left of Gordon Wells." He took off his headphones.

Jesse said, "Thanks for seeing us on such short notice."

"Nonsense." After shaking hands, Gordon said, "Mr. Croxford, thanks to Jesse, I feel like I know a little about you and your wife. Jesse tells me you're a Rhodesian war hero. Says, you saved his life."

"Jesse likes to exaggerate," Rigby said with a wink.

"How are things in Zimbabwe these days?" Gordon asked.

"Great people, shitty government, end of story."

"Like most places in the world. I understand your wife practices medicine in Africa. Wish I could meet her someday. Sadly, I'm running on borrowed time. Boy, am I ever. And you, Mr. Mahoney, I'd say you're from a southern state. Kentucky or maybe Tennessee."

"Kentucky."

"Are you married?"

"I'm separated."

His daughter appeared balancing drinks on a serving tray.

"You've met my daughter. Guess what, honey? Mr. Mahoney isn't married." His voice tailed off when he realized his daughter's irritation, but his smile broadened.

"For God's sake, don't you ever give up," Laura said. "I apologize for my father's tawdry antics."

"I reserve the right to be tasteless. After all, I *am* in my twilight years." He laughed heartily.

He waited for his daughter to leave the room. "My daughter's the best-kept secret in Key West. As much as I love this town, it's no place to find a husband—too many queens." His earthy laugh made him wheeze. He covered his mouth.

"Jesse told me a little about why you're here. I'm not sure I can help you. Before you tell me your story, you should know why I was forced to resign from the CIA. I worked for the agency for nineteen years —mostly operations overseas —security clearances and all that spooky nonsense. After my wife died, I underwent what I like to call an identity crisis. Like some others who shall remain anonymous, I didn't hide in the proverbial closet. My superiors thought I imposed a security risk. I could've sued, but that would've validated their antiquated logic. So, there you have it. The floor is all yours, Mr. Mahoney."

Sean told him about his Hong Kong episode. When he described his experience at Fu's brothel, Gordon interrupted him. "As it says in the Good Book, 'Let him who is without sin cast the first stone'. We're all sinners, Mr. Mahoney. Even me, now and again." He chuckled this time without wheezing.

Sean deferred to Rigby to describe the altercation at the marina. Gordon closed his eyes and locked his hands as in prayer. Sean tried to speak, but Gordon stopped him. Beads of sweat dotted his forehead. It was apparent that he was in a great deal of pain. When the throbbing subsided, he continued. "Two things make my impending death so inconvenient; unsatisfied curiosity and leaving my daughter. The morphine makes me groggy. I hate living like a zombie. I almost forgot, Jesse, take a look at my new *vandaceuos.*" He pointed with pride at a purple orchid in full flower.

"This is just a suggestion. You can take it or leave it. I'd move your yacht to a more public marina if I were you."

"Are you serious?" Sean asked.

Rigby interjected. "As they say in Africa, 'He who drinks at the same waterhole ends up in the lion's belly.'"

"It's just a precaution. Gentlemen, like I said before, I'm not sure I can help you. Let's see what my inquiries uncover. Now then, Mr. Mahoney, I need a special favor."

"Name it."

"Take my daughter out for dinner. Laura's been cooped up with me for six months. God knows, she deserves a pardon."

"Are you sure she's interested?" Sean asked.

"You get back here at eight. I'll handle my end."

Sean took Laura to a seaside restaurant. They ate dinner outside under a giant sycamore tree. Waves lapping against the seawall scented the air with a clean briny smell. Shrimp boats moving on the horizon twinkled like fireflies. Moonlight filtering through the branches made dancing silhouettes on their table. It was a romantic setting.

Failed relationships made them both wary. From the moment they sat down, they were searching for reasons why they should never see each other again. Their pointless talking was so awkward; they couldn't wait for the evening to end.

The second bottle of Chardonnay loosened their inhibitions. Laura bridged the impasse by asking Sean about the television business. She leaned toward him with obvious interest. He described a recent assignment, but it ended on a sour note when he mentioned his divorce and his repugnance for lawyers. More silent interludes wet-blanketed the already prickly atmosphere, until finally, Sean asked in desperation, "So, tell me about your father?"

"Well, what can I say? He's the kindest man I've ever known and the smartest. As you can tell, he's dying. I don't know what I'll do when he's gone." Her eyes moistened. She looked away.

"Any brothers or sisters?" he asked.

"One brother. He disowned our father after our mother died."

She seemed uncomfortable. "What about your friend from Africa? He seems quiet."

"Rigby? He's the quintessential warrior lost without a war. My sister's insanely in love with him. Wish I were more like him. Don't tell him I said that."

She shook her head. "Mum's the word."

"You haven't told me about yourself," said Sean.

"Me? There's not much to tell, really. Did my father tell you he was recruited right out of Yale law school?" She stopped to dab her eye with a tissue. "The CIA was his life. He lost his wife, his career and his son. My father doesn't have an ounce of bitterness in him. I'll never forgive them for what they did to him."

She tossed her hair back and looked intensely at him. In the candle light, her tearing eyes gave tantalizing reflections. My God, she's stunning. Maybe not as beautiful as Kathy, but much more wholesome, he thought. Her vulnerabilities stirred Sean's interest. For a split second, they were lost in each other's gaze. He hid his wedding band under the table and looked away afraid she would discover his thoughts. But then his reality resurfaced. I don't need you in my life, not right now, he thought.

Laura studied him critically. The salt-and-pepper hair means he's fiftyish. Not as physically fit as my ex-husband, which means he's probably not as self-absorbed. But then how could anyone be as self-centered. Better not get involved, she thought.

"How come you got divorced?" Sean asked, out of the blue. He realized his question was thoughtless, but it was too late for a retraction.

She seemed surprised by his bluntness. "I won't bore you with the details about how I caught my ex cheating on me. Let's just say, he'd screw a fire hydrant if it were possible."

"Did you look the other way for a long time?" he asked.

"I did for awhile, fool that I am." She blushed and then she retaliated with just a touch of teasing in her voice. "What about your wife? Was she having an affair?"

"Kathy? Heavens, no. At least, I don't think so." He grinned ruefully.

Sean had a flashback. He saw himself dancing with his wife at some late night dance club in New York. He was slightly out of step. It was late and he was tired, but his wife insisted on staying. I looked like an old fool, he thought. He ended the embarrassing thought by changing the subject. "Like your dad, I also went to Yale."

"I graduated from Georgetown."

"Did you ever work?" he asked without thinking again.

His question flushed her complexion. "Of course, I worked. Still do, in fact." She was visibly offended.

"Doing?"

Laura fortified herself with another sip of wine, smiled slyly and then she said, "Are you sure you wanna go there?"

"Don't tell me you're an attorney?" Sean grimaced like he had heartburn.

"For a D.C. firm. I'm on a leave of absence."

"Open mouth, insert foot." He smiled feebly.

She attempted to lighten his embarrassment. "When I went through my divorce, I felt the same way about lawyers."

"What kind of law do you practice?"

"Corporate, mostly. My college friends majored in finding a husband. Now, they're asking themselves, 'why?' I needed a way to pay the bills. At the time, law school seemed like a good option."

Sean buried his clichéd emotions. He sidetracked the conversation in another direction. "Has your father told you why we came to see him?"

"My father never talks about anything someone tells him in confidence, despite what those assholes at the CIA think. I haven't the foggiest idea."

He outlined his Hong Kong experience. He gave her an abbreviated cleaned-up version of what happened at Madam Fu's and his subsequent firing.

"You're not a sexual deviant, are you?" she asked smiling.

"I don't think so." He also smiled.

"Too bad," she said. "You do know I'm kidding."

He nodded awkwardly. He told her more about Nelson Chang and the Arabs. Without warning, a cold chill ran down the back of Sean's neck. What had been germinating in the back of his mind reappeared. His voice became sterile. "Let's get out of here."

15

Hong Kong

The Honeyguide had undergone some changes. Priceless masterpieces were replaced by time-zone clocks. Antique furniture was exchanged for utilitarian desks. Bundles of wire crisscrossed the teak decks. New global satellite antennas adorned the ship's masthead. Technicians installed direct links to the world's major banks and the exchanges. If Chang implemented his investment terrorism, he would execute it from his yacht.

Chang hired young security traders. He had them ferried to and from the Honeyguide every day. Under his tutelage they worked tirelessly, back-testing possible hedge and arbitrage scenarios. They never questioned his authority—to do so would be considered ill-mannered by Asian standards.

Reinvesting China's sovereign funds would disrupt the world's financial markets. But by the time the world's financial community got wind of China's stratagem, it would be too late. As Chang made his preparations, he remained skeptical about the terrorists having procured an atomic weapon and their ability to execute an attack. Half of his doubt was about to end.

On the tenth of April, Nelson Chang received the following message written in Arabic:

> Sir:
> Be advised that the item in question is ready
> for your inspection on the fourteenth of April
> at precisely 1400 hours GMT at longitude: 76
> degrees, 47 minutes west and latitude: 18
> degrees, 1 minute north. Listening on 122.5
> you will receive instructions concerning your
> final destination. May Allah protect you
> during your travels.
> God is great.

As one of the wealthiest men in the world, Chang was always manic about being kidnapped. He would fly to the initial fix and continue as the instructions dictated. Giving his pilot permission to land was another matter. The Arabs knew Chang would be wary. To minimize his anxiety, they sent him the following communiqué. A solid gold scimitar and a matching diamond embroidered sheath accompanied the following note:

Sir:
General Muhammad Obon will accompany
you on your journey. He will be unarmed and
as such, you are responsible for his security.
We hope this lessens your natural
apprehension. Please accept this gift as a sign
of our good faith.
Allahu Akbar

Chang's Gulfstream departed Hong Kong right on time. The transpacific flight plan listed San Francisco as a refueling stop with Kingston, Jamaica, as the final destination. The passenger manifest included the Sudanese general and Chang's two bodyguards. The nuclear physicist, Dr. Ming Soong, was a last minute addition believing he'd been hired as a consultant for a nuclear power plant project on the island of Jamaica. Chang would use the flying time to inform Soong about the real reason for his inclusion.

16

Key West

Gordon Wells's old colleagues at the CIA treated him like he had leprosy. His investigation of the Hong Kong incident was blocked at every turn. After exhausting all of his resources, Wells surreptitiously shared Rigby Croxford's opinion that Sean had watched too many spy movies.

With Gordon's prodding, Sean took Laura back to the same seaside restaurant for dinner.

Unlike their first date, the atmosphere was cordial, and they were the last ones to leave. After dinner, they walked on a deserted beach. The night air was chilled by a distant thunderhead. Low-flying wispy clouds partially screened the moon. A jagged bolt of lightning illuminated her face. He kissed her on the cheek. She melted into his arms and kissed him.

"What're you thinking about?" she asked.

It took him a while to answer her. "Nothing important. Just stuff."

She pulled herself closer to him and rested her head on his chest.

"I have to fly to New York next week," he whispered in her ear.

"You do, huh?" She pulled away from him and stared into the night.

They both started to talk at the same time. She deferred to him. "It's about my divorce."

"That's right, you're still married." She thought for a moment and then she said, "I think I've thought of a way to shed some light on your obsession."

"Please be more specific. I have an obsessive disorder." He smiled alone.

"It's about your Hong Kong experience."

He smiled luridly.

"Not that, you sex fiend. I mean what you overheard."

"For a second, I thought you..."

"I know what you thought. Let's go."

*   *   *

They found Gordon dozing in his wheelchair in front of a snowy television. He yawned and mumbled, "Damn lightning interrupted the nightly news. How was dinner?"

Laura kneeled down in front of her father. "I've been thinking. This is probably a stupid idea. What does the Agency hate most?"

"You mean, besides a nosy excommunicated agent."

"Yes, besides that."

"I give up. I'm riveted with anticipation."

"They hate any kind of publicity."

"Okay, they hate publicity. And where, may I ask, are you going with this?"

"What if Sean met with this agent Barrett and tells him he's working on a freelance documentary about Nelson Chang. Sean, you said by now he knows you were fired. The new piece is about what really happened or at least Barrett's version of what happened. According to Barrett, what you heard was an attempted swindle. If anything, the way he handled your coming forward shines a favorable light on both Barrett and the damn CIA."

"Before you get carried away, I believe agent Barrett. Case closed."

"Then how do you explain those men at the marina?" she asked.

"A random event. Apart from what the leftwing whackos think, the CIA doesn't get involved in domestic surveillance. For one thing, our Constitution forbids it," Gordon said.

"You always said a guarantee by the CIA guarantees there is no guarantee. God, I hate those bastards," said Laura.

"Sean, you must excuse my daughter. She's a bitter woman."

"You're damn right I'm bitter."

"Sweetheart, just remember a career with the CIA is like having an affair with a seductive mistress. It doesn't always end on a happy note."

Sean said, "Gordon, I know what I overheard. If those Arabs were lying, they deserve Oscars."

Her father shook his head, but he didn't argue. It was a while before he spoke again. "I guess there's no harm in trying it. If Barrett believes your so-called Arab plot has any legs, he'll do his best to dissuade you from doing this

fictitious segment. But I don't think he will."
Gordon was silent a moment before asking, "Sean, did
you move that yacht like I suggested?"

"Not yet. So, you don't think this thing's a figment of
my imagination?"

Gordon shook his head. "I wouldn't go that far. It's no
secret that the CIA has had dealings with Nelson Chang.
But to link him with this, this cock-and-bull story, is a
stretch. I will say this much, he's an unscrupulous
bastard."

"Chang can't be all bad. When I interviewed him in
Hong Kong, he told me he bought his adoptive parents an
English estate. He said, thanks to him, they lived out their
lives as millionaires."

Gordon looked alarmed. "Nelson Chang was adopted
by one of the wealthiest families in Great Britain. He
didn't buy an estate or anything else for those
unfortunate people."

"What happened to them?" Laura asked.

"They were murdered." Her father added, "I know
what you're both thinking."

"Which is?" asked Sean.

"Was the murder case ever solved? The answer is no.
And before you ask, Chang was never a suspect."

"Chang's mother was also murdered," said Sean.

Laura raised an eyebrow. "Just the utter randomness
of the universe, I suppose?"

Her father sighed openly. "Counselor, the evidence is
circumstantial, at best. Now then, how about letting an
old man get some sleep."

"Aye, aye, captain." Laura saluted.

"Sean, before you go—what was the name of Chang's
yacht again?"

"The Honeyguide. Why?"

"No reason, really. Just curious."

Laura kissed her father goodnight.

Gordon Wells waited for them to leave the room before booting up his computer. He punched the word, "honeyguide". He expected to see a picture of Chang's yacht, but instead he saw a photograph of a brown bird. He read the following ornithological description:

> Honeyguides lay their eggs in other bird species'
> nests. The newly hatched chicks kill their fellow
> nestlings by pecking them to death. As a result,
> the chicks are reared by their unsuspecting foster
> parents. When food is scarce, the larger honeyguide
> fledglings sometimes eat their adoptive parents.

JAMES GARDNER

17

Sean got Harry Rosen's permission to move his Hatteras to another marina. The dock-master told them the best place to hire a part-time captain was at Cracker Jack's Saloon on Stock Island. He neglected to tell them that some unemployed captains were drug smugglers or worse.

A person needed determination to find Cracker Jack's. The signage had letters missing. A row of Harley Davisons blocked the front entrance. Sean and Rigby entered through a side door and sat down at the bar. They received unfriendly glances from four men playing pool. A rail-thin woman sat alone at the other end of the bar nursing a beer. She had a black eye and a swollen lip. Her hair was blond, but her roots told a different story. Glassy-eyed fish-mounts covered the walls. A wobbling ceiling fan moved hot air.

When Sean mentioned to the bartender that they wanted to hire a captain, the man shouted, "Hey, Luther, you lookin' for work?"

Luther James's arms and neck were completely covered by tattoos. He was built like a fireplug with a neck so short, his earlobes rested on his shoulders. He wore a diamond earring in one ear. A heavy brow over-shadowed shifty eyes. His fingernails were blackened by engine grease and fish blood.

"What kinda work?" Luther asked. He ejected a squirt of tobacco juice into an empty Budweiser beer can.

"We need someone to help us move a yacht."

"Ain't no doubt about it, boss, I'm your man. Where would I be moving her to? Before you tell me—I get three hundred bucks a day plus extra if we're breakin' the law. Hey, I'm only kiddin' about the illegal shit." His expression revealed that he wasn't kidding.

"We're docked at Island Marina. We'd like a more public..."

"Why hell, I could tie her up next to my boat over yonder." He pointed at a black speedboat powered by four outboards. That way, I could keep an eye on her. If ya get my drift. Named her after Dale Earnhardt. The Miss Earnhardt can outrun anything that floats. I mean anything, and that includes the Key West pigs. Know what I mean?" He suspended his snickering to discharge more tobacco spittle into the can.

"We're thinking a little less rustic."

Luther gave them a sideways glance. "Okay, how about Oceanside?"

"Will you need a mate? We'll be out of town for a..."

"Shit, my lady friend's all the help I need." He winked at the woman seated at the bar. She smiled carefully around a discolored front tooth.

"Call me when you want that boat moved. I'm in the book. Ask anyone in this town about Luther James, they'll set you straight."

"Thanks, Luther. We'll be in touch."

Rigby and Sean stepped outside into the sunlight and looked at each. "Think we should interview another captain?" asked Rigby.

Sean said, "Oh, I don't know, Luther seems competent enough. Wonder if Harry's yacht insurance covers theft."

18

Laura and Sean woke up with sunlight sneaking into their cabin. She rested her head on his chest. He kissed her on the cheek and whispered, "I hope you liked it as much as I did."

"What on earth are you talking about?"

"You know."

"Oh, that. I was half asleep. I guess it was all right."

He lifted her face. "You *are* joking, aren't you?"

"Would I kid you?"

"Careful doctor, your patient has issues."

"Aww, what's a matter—did I ruffle your male ego?" She said this imitating baby-talk.

"What ego? I'm an unemployed loser. I'm getting divorced in three days, which means I'll be destitute. If this were eighteenth century England, I'd be locked up in a debtor's prison."

"That means we've only got three days of adultery left." She giggled and tried to get away. He grabbed her wrist and pulled her down on top of him.

"I pour my heart out. What do you do, you make fun of me."

She kissed him on the check. "You know what they say, 'Laughter is an orgasm triggered by the intercourse of sense and nonsense.'"

"God, I love it when you talk dirty," he whispered.

It was smooth sailing for the next two days, but as Sean's divorce hearing grew closer, he became more distant and less attentive. Notwithstanding his assurances to the contrary, Laura realized that Sean was still in love with his wife. It all came to a head at dinner during their last night together in Key West. The evening started out well enough, but too much wine loosened their tongues. A petty disagreement turned into a bigger one and then silence.

Without warning, Laura asked, "So, how's Kathy?" Her eyes narrowed as she waited.

"Kathy who?" He squirmed nervously.

"Who the hell do ya think? Your wife, that's who."

Treading carefully, Sean asked, "What brought her name up?" He searched desperately for their waitress. He needed more wine in a hurry.

"You called her, didn't you." Her face hardened. Angry wrinkles outlined her mouth.

"I don't know what you're talking about." Sean fortified himself with the last of his wine.

"Why the hell wouldn't you call her, she's your wife, for Christ's sake. I must be crazy. You probably think about her when you're in bed with me."

"That's not true and you know it. Laura, please don't do this."

"I saw her picture in Vogue. If I lived in Kentucky, I'd be old enough to be her mother. I can't compete with her, I really can't." She appeared to be barely holding back tears.

"Kathy, there's no need to..." He hesitated realizing he'd mistakenly used his wife's name. "Oops," he said placing his hand on her arm.

Laura eyed him with frustration. She pushed his hand away saying, "Aha! I think that just about says it all, doesn't it. My father warned me about moving too fast. God damn him, anyway. He's always right. Sean, will you do me a favor?"

"Anything, just name it."

"Please let me out of your life." Tears came without the sobbing.

"But..." She stopped him by placing her fingers over his lips.

Regret left him speechless. He thought about saying something clever, but it was too late. He watched her walk away and did nothing to stop her.

She looked back at him. Her smile was sad.

JAMES GARDNER

19

Over Jamaica

Nelson Chang studied the crystal ice flowers forming in the corners of the cabin window. From 40,000 feet, the tops of Jamaica's Blue Mountains looked like anthills floating on a velvety white sea of cotton. The pilot was completing his second circling turn when General Obon handed Chang a note containing latitude and longitude coordinates. As Chang walked forward to the cockpit, he inwardly congratulated the jihadists. He had worried about receiving instructions via the radio. This would lessen the chance of eavesdropping. His South African copilot typed the coordinates into the global positioning system. The new heading would take them to Central America.

Two hours later, Chang's Gulfstream touched down at the Belize City International Airport. The pretext of their unscheduled visit was that they were wealthy investors interested in purchasing a seaside resort. Belize government officials were bribed. The people in charge complied with the request for anonymity. There was no formal greeting at the airport. The group bypassed the usual immigration and customs delays. They were whisked away in a limousine book-ended by two military jeeps.

The coastal highway runs south through endless saltwater marshes. A few times, they got glimpses of the Caribbean Sea, but mostly they saw only mangroves. Low tide yielded a stench of rotting marigolds but it was no match for General Obon's body odor. Chang used an embroidered handkerchief to cover his nose.

The further they traveled away from the capital, the fewer villages they encountered. For the last few miles, the road was reduced to a corrugated shell-rock path. The road ended at a security gate marking the entrance to a seaside resort. The sign read: Welcome to Emerald Seas. The gate was manned by two security guards and a man wearing reflective sunglasses and a brightly flowered shirt. The nod of recognition told Chang that the loudly dressed man and General Obon knew each other.

Chang, Dr. Soong and General Obon were escorted to adjoining seaside chateaus. A razor-wired security fence protected the compound. Armed sentries and guard dogs patrolled the outer perimeter.

Chang noted an island freighter; the Caribbean Moon from Monrovia was anchored offshore. A guard told him that the container ship had been impounded for unpaid import taxes. Chang suspected that what he had traveled halfway around the world to see was onboard that ship.

With dusk sliding into the Caribbean Sea, Soong, Chang and Obon sat on a veranda sipping Champagne. True to form, the general became inebriated. Chang ordered his bodyguards to escort the general back to his room. Obon objected at first, but he relented.

Chang and Soong's tête-à-tête was frivolous. Lapping surf muted their voices. Even so, Chang demanded that Dr. Soong use Mandarin as an added precaution. Fortified by alcohol, Soong redirected their conversation by recounting the destruction of Hiroshima by the Americans in 1945. Chang had indentified the weapon to be inspected as a 20 kiloton uranium-235 fission bomb, which was larger than the first bomb dropped on Japan. Soong assumed the detonation would be at ground level, thereby losing some shockwave destruction. He mentioned that 70,000 Japanese civilians were vaporized by the 7200 degree fireball. Another 100,000 inhabitants died slow agonizing deaths from radiation sickness. The 700 mph pressure wave flattened 90 percent of the city's buildings. He concluded by saying that Japan had been on the verge of surrendering and that dropping two atomic bombs on helpless civilians was barbaric. Soong pushed back his steel-rimmed spectacles and waited for Chang's response. What he heard shocked him.

"As far as I'm concerned, your attempt to evoke my sympathy falls on deaf ears."

"But surely, you don't condone killing innocent civilians?"

"Let me ask you something. Tell me, doctor, how many innocent Chinese civilians did the Imperial Japanese military slaughter in the Second World War?"

Chang shook his head as if he was warding off an unpleasant recollection.

"Barbarity's immoral in any form." said Soong.

"Doctor, I hope you know more about nuclear physics than you do about human behavior." Chang was visibly annoyed by Soong's sermon.

Their standoff was short-lived. Soong remarked that New York City had a much larger population than Hiroshima and Nagasaki. He paused, waiting for Chang's reaction to his conjecture.

Chang clasped his hands together and thought for a moment. He stared past Soong at the rising moon. "Doctor, I have paid you to perform a specific task. I must warn you in the strongest terms against voicing your uneducated guesses."

Soong stammered. "Yes, of course, I...I only."

Chang showed more irritation by interrupting him again. "I have no interest in your opinion. How long will it take you to complete the inspection?"

Soong refused eye contact saying, "One hour or less. I need a few tools and the radiation portal monitor you provided. I must examine the triggering mechanism and the enriched uranium sphere and..."

"Good. I've just been informed that they're waiting for you on the beach. I'm eager to hear your evaluation. My desire is to leave Belize as soon as possible. Now, if you'll excuse me."

Dr. Soong watched Chang limp away. He breathed a sigh of relief. Chang's rudeness was gnawing on his nerves. The cool breeze made him shiver. He yearned for his Beijing apartment and the safety of his wife's bed.

It was slack tide. The lack of current made the Caribbean Moon pitch and roll like a fat woman having sex on a waterbed. Getting aboard was difficult for Soong.

He was an old man with no sea legs. He had to be lifted over the gunnels in a boson's chair. The smell of diesel added to Soong's queasiness. He puked three times before he reached the cargo containers. The Arab deckhands enjoyed Soong's sickness. When a man offered him a Turkish cigarette, he ran to the railing and dry-heaved. This added to their amusement.

He was so lightheaded by the time he started the inspection, he could hardly stand up. The enclosed cargo container was stifling. The smell of the sweating Arabs added to his purgatory. Dangling lights illuminated a large torpedo-shaped device with ventral fins. He felt woozy.   When Soong squatted to examine the inscriptions, he broke wind. He pushed the Arabs out of way and burst out of the container.

"I've seen enough. Get me on dry land."

The time passed slowly for Chang. He paced like a caged leopard. He craned his neck to see, but heard the whining outboard before he saw the launch nudge up on the beach. Dr. Soong and the man wearing the loud Hawaiian shirt walked out of the darkness. Chang handed Soong a glass of Champagne as a peace offering.

"Doctor, what did you find out?" Chang's eagerness caused him to rock forward on his walking stick. He arrested his twitching eye socket with his free hand.

Stinging from being rebuffed earlier, Soong chastised Chang by stalling.

"That leaky rust bucket isn't seaworthy. I've never been sicker in my life."

"I didn't bring you halfway around the world to do a marine survey. Was there an atomic device onboard or not?"

Soong postponed his answer by taking a protracted sip of Champagne. After inhaling on a cigarette, he overstated his inspection by saying, "The gun-type assembly method indicates the weapon was manufactured around fifty years ago. The inscriptions are in Russian. The device is old technology. It's..."

Chang interrupted him by demanding, "Yes, yes, but will the weapon detonate?"

Soong continued his lecturing. "Well, it could, assuming strict sequence measures are adhered to. In terms of external damage, it's important to distinguish between detonations and deflagrations where the exothermic wave is subsonic and maximum pressures..."

"Assuming the proper procedures are followed, will the damn thing explode or not?" Unconsciously, Chang raised his cane.

Fearing the cane, Soong blurted, "It will, without question."

Chang lowered his walking stick. He was taken aback, but faked his indifference. He looked out into the tar-black night. At that moment he felt the weight of China's destiny.

20

April 21

Sean and Rigby waited in the taxi line at the La Guardia Airport. Sean checked his phone messages. He ignored messages from Harry Rosen and his wife. The last call was from Laura, which he redialed. "God, I'm glad you called."

Laura disregarded his warm greeting. "What was the captain's name? The man you hired to move your boss's yacht."

"Luther James. Why?"

"He was found floating in the Island Marina basin."

Sean paused. "He was dead?"

"He sure as hell wasn't snorkeling. The Monroe County Sheriff's Department says his death was drug-related. And I don't mean he died from an overdose."

"Luther looked pretty tough."

"Not tough enough. They had to identify him by his tattoos. I'll call when I find out more. Take care of yourself, Sean."

"Laura..." There was only a dial tone.

Having overheard some of the conversation, Rigby said, "Sounds like I won't be headed back to Zimbabwe anytime soon."

Instead of answering, Sean nodded.

The line of people waiting for taxis was two-blocks long and growing longer by the minute. A strike by the New York City cabbies had brought city transportation to a standstill. Sean replayed more messages as he shuffled forward at a snail's pace. The first message was from his wife, Kathy, which he deleted. The second message was equally depressing; it was his attorney offering inane legal advice. The last message was from Harry Rosen wishing him good luck with his final settlement hearing.

Sensing Sean's despair, Rigby asked, "Are you all right?"

"Huh. I'm fine. At this rate, we may never get into the city. Let's see if we can find a Gypsy cab."

They walked against the traffic. The third car they encountered was a raked Cadillac Coup Deville. Lavon and Rigby locked eyes. Lavon turned to Jamal. "Well, déjà-fuckin-vu, it's that African dude."

"Say what?" Jamal said.

"You know, bro, the honky who bitch-slapped you."

Jamal shouted, "Shit. Lock the fuckin' doors." He was too late, Rigby jumped into the backseat. Sean followed suit.

"Remember me?" Rigby asked.

"Damn right, I remember you," Jamal said rubbing his jaw. "Now, get the fuck outta my car."

"C'mon, man, let bygones be bygones," Rigby said.

"You get your ass bygone." Jamal looked straight ahead.

Sean interceded. "Okay, name your price."

"There ain't no price. I said, get outta my car."

"Would you drive us into the city for, say, five hundred dollars?"

Jamal studied Sean in the rearview mirror for a moment. "Shit, for that kinda money, I'd carry you on my fuckin' back."

"Okay, someplace between zero and five hundred, you and I are gonna cut a deal."

After intense haggling, Sean and Jamal agreed to three hundred dollars. On the drive into Manhattan, Sean hired them for three more days at the same rate.

The next day, at eleven o'clock sharp, Jamal and Lavon reported for duty in front of Sean's Fifth Avenue apartment building. Rigby and Sean climbed into the backseat of their Cadillac.

"And how are you two fine-looking gentlemen doing on this glorious morning?" Rigby asked.

Jamal grunted, "I don't do happy this fuckin' early." Lavon whispered something under his breath.

Sean and Rigby met Robert Barrett for lunch at the Athletic Club. During lunch, Barrett and Rigby got into a heated discussion about the differences between rugby and American football. When their conversation diverted to the military, the friction eased. Finally, Sean said to Barrett. "Rigby had contact with Nelson Chang in Africa."

"Oh, how did that come about?" Barrett asked. He tried to represent a lack of interest, but his eyes darted, telling a different story.

"Chang was selling arms to the Sudanese militias," Rigby said.

Barrett acted like he wanted to hear more details, but Sean stopped the dialogue by taking out a notebook and a ballpoint. "I'm putting the finishing touches on a new short about Nelson Chang. I'd appreciate your input."

"I'm confused. I thought you were fired?" Barrett said.

"I presold this piece to another network. You'll be happy to know you're depicted as a dedicated professional." Sean poised with paper and pen preparing to take dictation.

"We're prohibited from doing unauthorized interviews. Think I could see your segment before it gets aired?" Barrett asked.

"Sorry, we don't do previews. What's the problem?"

"Inflaming the public can have unintended consequences." Barrett added, "Off the record, we're having delicate negotiations with the Chinese government."

"Concerning? Off the record, of course."

"I'm not at liberty to say."

"It's a documentary, not the Holy Grail."

"Mr. Mahoney, forty percent of Americans believe in UFOs."

"Our target market is the other sixty percent." Sean's smile was unreturned.

The parting atmosphere was uncomfortable. Sean offered Barrett an olive branch by saying that he would try to send him a copy of the documentary as soon as it was available.

"Well, whatdaya think?" Sean asked Rigby after they were alone.

"Barrett shit in his pants."

"Yeah. So?" Sean said. "Will he take steps to stop me?"

"You can bet on it," Rigby said.

21

Sean was reconciled to losing his New York apartment. The day before his final settlement hearing, Rigby helped him box-up a few keepsakes and his clothes. He was practicing his putting stroke when his cell phone rang. "Mr. Mahoney, you're in luck. I got them goods we spoke about."

"Who is this?"

"It's Carmine."

"You're too late, Carmine. My court date's tomorrow morning."

"Better late than never. Meet me at Paddy's in one hour. Remember, no cash means you don't want what I got and I got plenty, pal. *Capishe*?"

Carmine was seated in a rear booth between the restrooms. His appearance was more disheveled than ever. He dispensed with the formalities. "Did you bring the cash?"

Sean took a manila envelope out of his coat pocket and tossed it on the table. "Aren't you gonna count it?"

Carmine fanned the bills like a deck of cards. He sniffed the money and swooned like he was smelling roses. "I trust you. Look, before I give you what I got, I wanna say something. Mr. Mahoney, you don't strike me as a violent person. You wouldn't do anything crazy, would you?"

"Like what?" Sean nervously twisted his wedding ring.

"Well, like shoot your wife and her fuckin' boyfriend. Oops, sorry 'bout that. That could get us both into hot water."

"I wouldn't shoot anyone, ever, under any circumstances." Sean felt the air being sucked out of his lungs. He felt lightheaded.

A long silence got longer. Carmine got Paddy's attention. He ordered his usual boilermaker.

"All right, then." He handed Sean a folder. "Sorry, it took me so long. Getting these was a real ball-buster. The douche bag lives in a Bronxville mansion with his wife and three kids but he rents a love crib on the upper Westside. If it makes you feel any better, he's been doin' this kinda shit for years. The trick was plantin' the cameras. Damn near got busted breakin' into his building. I'd love to be a fly on the wall when Ackerman sees these."

"Who?" Sean asked, not connecting the dots.

The first photograph was grainy, but Sean recognized his wife and a man entering an apartment building. Each picture was more sexually explicit than the one before it. The man's identity still didn't register. Sean felt like he'd been punched in the gut.

[134]

"Ackerman. Your wife's screwing her attorney, Morris Ackerman. Like I said, he's been fuckin' his clients for years, in more ways than one, if you get my drift." His words became indistinguishable and then faded away altogether as he realized Sean's anguish.

Sean washed his face with his hands and sighed. "Carmine, I'd like to be alone."

"Sure, I understand. There ain't negatives. So use them wisely."

Paddy showed up with Carmine's drinks. Sean said, "I'll have the same."

Sean shook his head. "I can't do it to her, I just can't."

Carmine stared at him openmouthed. "What? Are you kidding me? You're home free. Hey, I busted my balls gettin' these." He nodded at the photographs. He tried to figure Sean's angle, but there wasn't one.

Finally, he said, "Ackerman stalked your wife. This ain't the first marriage he's destroyed, and it won't be the last. In the end, he'll fleece her like he done the others. You get a chance—you ask her who made the original contact. He only does high-end divorces. Look, I'm sorry it went down this way, but it is what it is. I hope everything works out for you, Mr. Mahoney. Good luck."

Carmine downed the whiskey and gulped the beer. He slipped out of the booth and headed for the exit. He stole a quick glimpse of Sean, shook his head and then he disappeared into the crowd outside.

Sean waited a long time before he ordered his next drink. As he reviewed his marriage, he knew his intuition had been right all along. His recent infidelity made it hard to condemn his wife. The focus of his bitterness was Morris Ackerman. You were screwing my wife and charging me a fortune at the same time, you prick.

His hands were trembling, but he managed to dial his cell phone. "I'd like to speak to Mr. Ackerman. This is Sean Mahoney. Tell him it's important."

Ackerman picked up immediately. "Mr. Mahoney, what can I do for you?"

Sean thought, well for one thing, you can stop screwing my wife. But he said, "Look, I'd like to get this divorce thing settled. Why don't you get the papers ready? I'll stop by and sign them."

There was silence on the line as Ackerman tried to figure out Sean's motive.

"I must inform you that this is highly irregular. Have you consulted with your attorney about your intention?" Ackerman sounded giddy now.

"We both know my attorney's a schmuck. Now, when can I sign those papers?"

"And you're in total agreement with the terms I set forth?"

"Absolutely."

"It just so happens, your wife's in my office this very minute. Can you get here in say, an hour?"

Sean thought, gee, imagine that, but he said, "I'll be there in thirty minutes."

"I'm glad you decided to treat Mrs. Mahoney with the dignity she deserves. There's no reason divorces can't be amicable."

Sean hung up and yelled, "Barkeep, make this one a double." He twisted off his ring and shoved it into his pocket.

Morris Ackerman wore elevator shoes with his Armani suit. His Palm Beach tan was too orange not to be chemically induced. Hair-plugs crisscrossed his scalp like rows of planted corn. An unwrinkled face hinted of plastic surgery. He looked at Sean over half-moon glasses perched on his perfect nose. Sean was ushered in by a bleached blond secretary. Kathy was seated in a high-backed wingchair next to Ackerman. They both looked triumphant and smug.

"Like I said on the telephone, Mr. Mahoney, it's unusual not to have both parties represented by counsel."

"Well, what can I say? I'm in an am... amicable mood," Sean said, fumbling the pronunciation. He grinned at his wife. She looked back at him with disdain.

"This is the final decree." Ackerman pushed forward a folder as thick as a Bible. "I'd like to go over the terms, just to make sure you understand what you're signing. My secretaries can act as witnesses."

Ackerman handed a duplicate to Sean's wife. He put his hand on her shoulder in a consoling, fatherly fashion. She placed her hand on top of his and smiled weakly. He patted her hand in a fake, "I feel your pain" gesture.

"Before I sign my life away, I'd like to speak to you both in private," Sean said.

"Regarding?" Ackerman inquired.

"Why not indulge me and find out."

Ackerman motioned to his secretaries to leave the room. "Please be brief, Mr. Mahoney. I have other appointments."

Sean lit a cigarette and exhaled a massive lungful of smoke.

Ackerman protested by paddling the air. "We have a no-smoking policy in this office."

"Is that right? Well, good for you." Sean expelled an even thicker cloud. "Okay, here's what I'm willing to do."

[137]

"Wait just a minute. What you're willing to do?" Ackerman echoed and then he added, "This isn't what we agreed to on the telephone."

"Listen up, Ackerman. I'll sign over the house in East Hampton, but I want the apartment. And there'll be no alimony. Kathy, you make more money than I do, or rather did, make. I'm presently unemployed, not that you give two shits."

"You're drunk," rebuked his wife. She looked crestfallen. This wasn't going the way she'd envisioned it would.

"As you might have guessed..." Sean belched and covered his mouth. "I've been celebrating." His grin was lopsided.

"Have you taken a complete leave of your senses?" Ackerman snapped. He pretended astonishment, but seeds of suspicion crept into his eyes.

"Oh, there's more, Ackerman. I'll expect a complete reimbursement of all legal bills. And I want you to pay off those blood-sucking forensic accountants."

"My God, you really are delusional." Ackerman pushed the intercom and shouted, "Miss Neuman, call security." He now had more Bronx in his voice than Upper Eastside.

"Before you have me thrown out—I think you'd better have a look at these." He let the photographs spill out onto Ackerman's desk.

There was only stunned silence.

Ackerman faked indifference. "How did you get these?" he asked blushing.

"Does it really matter? Kinda gives new meaning to the old adage, a picture is worth a thousand words, wouldn't you say?"

"Mr. Mahoney, blackmail's a serious crime, not to mention breaking and entering." Spitballs appeared in the corners of Ackerman's mouth.

"He's bluffing." Kathy snarled. Sean was surprised by the loathing in her eyes.

"Am I? Two other sets are ready to be mailed out. One set's addressed to your wife in Bronxville, Ackerman. Let's see how you like getting hosed for a change. Another set's going to the New York Bar Association."

"He wouldn't dare. Well, don't just sit there, do something," his wife snapped.

"There's nothing I can do," Ackerman said. He put his hand on her arm. She jerked free and snarled, "Bullshit. I'll hire another lawyer."

"Oh, no you won't. You'll be a good little girl and you'll do exactly as I say. Now, sit down and be quiet. Mr. Mahoney, I'll have the signed agreement delivered to your attorney within the hour."

"Kathy, ask him how many divorcees he's swindled? You were setup from the get-go."

"Mahoney, you have no idea who you're dealing with." Ackerman turned to Kathy and said, "Obviously, your husband's psychotic."

Sean could feel Ackerman's hatred, but he forced a grin. "Am I? Good luck, Kathy. You're damn sure gonna need it."

He heard his wife screaming after he shut the door. Ackerman's secretaries flinched when they heard something hit the wall in their boss's office.

Lavon, Jamal and Rigby were waiting in the Cadillac. When Sean saw them, he gave them thumbs up.

"It looks like you nailed the bastard," Rigby said to Sean.

"Ackerman's had better days. After I pick up my divorce papers, I'm buying you guys dinner."

"Ya know, I could get used to this kinda life," said Lavon.

"It would mean giving up your life in crime," said Rigby. "Which is good, 'cause you're a much better chauffeur than a mugger."

"Now, how did I know you'd have to mention that shit?" Lavon bumped fists with Rigby.

The Frenchified maitre d' looked like he'd been starched in arrogance. He raised an eyebrow when he saw Lavon and Jamal. Lavon was decked out in a pink jumpsuit and a matching scarlet fedora. Jamal walked with a rakish hip-hop swagger.

When the maitre d' recognized Sean, his worry seemed to ease. "I put you and your guests in the back, Mr. Mahoney."

"I'd prefer my usual table upfront."

"Very good, sir." The man looked as repulsed as a father changing his first diaper.

The celebrating continued after dinner. Sean hoisted a brandy sniffer "I'd like to propose a toast to ex-wives and their divorced husbands—may they never meet again."

"Cheers." Rigby clicked glasses with Lavon.

Sean's cell phone rang. It was Robert Barrett. He held up his hand. When the call ended, he explained that Barrett had asked him to delay the airing of his make-believe documentary. He cited the ongoing negotiations between China and the United States as the reason.

"Barrett made it sound like I was Benedict Arnold if I didn't cancel. Now, do you believe me?" Sean asked.

"At this point, I can't think of a reason not to."

"Where do we go from here?"

"Back to Key West, I reckon. Wonder if Jesse can get me a weapon," said Rigby. Lavon and Jamal nodded their approval.

"You mean a gun?" Sean asked

"Unless you think a club would be more effective."

"Sometimes, you sound so God damned dramatic."

"I live in Africa, where not getting killed is a profession. That guy in Key West didn't stick his finger in my ribs. And there's what happened to Luther James. Besides, I feel naked without a weapon."

Sean placed his hand on his brother-in-law's shoulder."God, I'm glad you're here."

"I better see if Jesse'll meet us at the airport."

22

Robert Barrett descended the gangway of a Learjet. He climbed into a chauffeur-driven black Ford Explorer. The hanger door reopened. The Ford disappeared into a drizzly Miami night. The door closed.

It's a one-hour drive from the International Airport to the Homestead Air Force Base. As Barrett rode through the rain-soaked streets, he thought about his pending meeting with the director of the Far East section.

Hardwick Harrington graduated from the Woodrow Wilson School of International and Public Affairs at Princeton. Harrington's late mother had married well and divorced better, not once, but three times. In spite of a large inheritance, Harrington lived on a modest farm in Virginia, where he bred Labrador Retrievers.

Security was heightened at Homestead. Entrance through the outer gate was obtained by showing identification credentials. Getting through the inner fence required passing a fingerprint scanner. Right of entry to a Quonset hut tucked away in a corner of the base was granted by someone on the inside pressing a button that opened the door.

"How was the flight?" Harrington sat on a sofa with a black Lab sleeping at his feet. His rimless spectacles were partially hidden by a bird's nest of white hair.

"It sure beats commercial." Barrett sat down.

"Sorry about the theatrics. I mean, making you land in Miami. We're trying not to draw undo attention to our presence here. Oprah, go say hello." The dog saddled over and put her chin on Barrett's knee.

"You're the first person to enter this hellhole in two weeks. We eat, sleep and defecate in this aluminum box. We're all going bonkers. What about the problem we discussed on the telephone?" Harrington elevated his eyebrows.

"I'm on it," Barrett answered.

"For our sakes, let's hope so. Three years of work. Millions we've invested. If we don't contain this, it could backfire and ruin everything."

"Sir, do you have any suggestions?" Barrett asked. "How far can I go?"

"Well, let's see. We've got this Cronkite wannabe and his brother-in-law sticking their noses under our tent. What are their names again?"

"Mahoney and Croxford."

"Now, I hear they've enlisted my old handler, Gordon Wells. Gordon got drummed out of the agency years ago. Rumor is the poor man's dying. Gordon needs to answer the call of his Maker. I know that sounds cruel, maybe too much so. But there's a lot at stake here."

"I understand," said Barrett.

[144]

"A security breach this late in the game would be a travesty. If you feel they're getting too close, you have my permission to do whatever's necessary to contain the damage. If you disagree, please say so."

"I agree, totally."

"Good. I'm counting on you, Bob. When this is over, we have to guard against any blowback. There can be no links back to us, at least for the time being."

Harrington's mind drifted as he listened to Barrett's assurances. He thought about how the assholes in State and the politicos on the Intelligence Committee would disavow any knowledge of the operation if it fails. Rats off a sinking ship, he thought.

"Now, how about a cigar before dinner? Don't pay attention to the label—they're as Cuban as Castro. I have them smuggled in from Guantanamo."

Harrington selected a cigar from the mahogany humidor on his desk. He dragged it under his nose and then carefully removed the band.

"There's something I want you to see." Harrington unfolded an aeronautical chart and spread it over his desk. He used his unlit cigar as a pointer. "This course line represents Nelson Chang's transpacific flight from Hong Kong to San Francisco. After refueling, he flew to this spot over Jamaica, before diverting to Belize City." He circumcised the cigar tip with his teeth and jettisoned it. He missed the wastepaper basket. Oprah ran over, sniffed the butt and sneezed.

"Two days later, he flew back to Hong Kong. So far, so good."

"What's he like, sir?"

"Nelson Chang? I've had dealings with the man for thirty years. I'm not sure anyone really knows him. I'll say one thing—the inscrutable bastard's a genius. Matching wits with him gives me migraines." Harrington pinched the bridge of his nose. "I'm told the helicopter crash took a toll on him, in more ways than one. Altering his medication is our ace in the hole."

Barrett asked, "What motivates Chang?"

"I'm not sure. It can't be money, not with his billions. Perhaps he wants his place in history. Thirty years in the intelligence business has left me with more questions than answers. Bob, you *do* know this could be a career-maker for you."

"And if we fail?"

"Think security guard at a shopping mall in Alaska."

"That bad?"

"I'm afraid so. Langley has a history of throwing people under the bus when shit happens. Lambs are sacrificed so that the wolves can go on living, as they say."

Harrington's cigar had expired. He coaxed it back with a match, and then extinguished the match with a wave. "This operation's my swan song. I spent the last thirty years on the seamy side of life. It's time to cleanse my soul."

"Sir, you've made your mark," Barrett said.

"I'd like to think so. Truth is—the public doesn't trust us. This country's got too many God damned conspiracy fruitcakes. In spite of the Warren Commission, most Americans believe we were involved in the Kennedy assassination. Can you imagine that? For Christ's sake, forty percent of Americans believe in UFOs."

Barrett stiffened as he spoke. "The country needs us."

Harrington shrugged. "No doubt about it. They want us to do our dirty work but don't want to hear the messy details. Our plan was to assassinate Bin Laden from the get-go. Now, we pretend we were forced to kill him. It's all bullshit. By the way, not killing him would have been the monumental fuckup of all times."

"In that case, the end certainly justified the means."

Harrington sighed openly. "We all know it's only a matter of time before the crazies detonate a bomb on American soil. Problem is we have to stop them with our hands tied. Odds are we'll eventually fail. When it happens, I hope I'm dead and buried. Sorry, I'm ranting. Let's eat dinner before I lose my appetite."

23

Hong Kong
Onboard the Honeyguide

N elson Chang gained the floor by tapping a gilded tumbler with his spoon. "Gentlemen, please be seated. I'd like to discuss the economy."

Two men seated at the table were members of the communist party's inner circle. Other attendees included the president of Petro China and the father of China's nuclear energy program, Dr. Ming Soong. Chang's longtime adversary, Dr. Fi Wong, chairman of China's redevelopment agency, sat at the other end of the table. Dr. Wong saw Chang as a symbol of capitalistic greed. Conversely, Chang viewed Wong as a hard-line communist holdover from the Red Guard era.

Chang waited for silence. I must make all of you my accomplices, he thought. He started by saying, "I hope each of you has taken the time to read my exposé on our economy. I heard a rumor that Dr. Wong believes my essay is the most important bathroom text ever published." His remark received muffled laughter from the group. Chang's rare smile was forced. He stared at Wong, who was, by now, showing the effects of the wine.

"In my opinion, our economy resembles a teetering house of cards, yet Dr. Wong—you continue to build colossal residential developments. Monuments to one man's ego. But without buyers, the cities are ghost towns."

Dr. Wong jumped to his feet. "Surely, Mr. Chang knows that to suspend construction could evoke a general strike and that might spark a civil unrest in the entire country!" Chang's stare caused him discomfort. He sat down and looked at the other men at the table for moral support, which some granted.

Chang wagged his finger at Wong. "Better to have civil unrest now and not total anarchy later. Unless we take Draconian measures soon, the dark day of reckoning is near. The seeds of inflation have been sown. Economic failures are systemic. Half of this country's bank loans are nonperforming. In truth, our economy is a festering boil ready to be lanced. Someday soon, we will be held responsible for our failings."

The carefully selected guests stared gloomily into their drinks. One man stared at the ceiling and another one picked his teeth. None of them looked at Chang.

Dr. Wong stood up. "In the United States, the forty richest men have accumulated more wealth than 160 million Americans. Is this what you want for China?"

Chang looked up from his notes and swept his audience with a steely glance. "How do you think the poorest Americans compare with our peasants?"

"You're one of the richest men in the world. What do you know about being poor?"

"Spoken like a loyal communist. My dear, Dr. Wong, I wasn't always rich. If it would please you, I can act contrite."

"A repentant Chang? Perish the thought." Wong's smile revealed silver-tipped incisors.

Wong asked, "I'm curious, would you care to tell us where you've invested your personal holdings?"

Chang felt the curious eyes of his guests assessing him. He delayed his response by requesting more drinks for his guests.

"As members of the advisory committee for the sovereign funds, all of you approved my decision to concentrate our investments in the United States. Unfortunately, my personal assets mirror the funds' holdings."

Chang's guests fidgeted nervously waiting for his explanation. Chang motioned for the waiters to leave the salon. He used the silence to review his notes.

"Gentlemen, I'm going to tell you a story that could alter world history. Each of you must decide about the legitimacy of my findings and devise a plan of action. I'm getting ahead of myself. Let me digress." Chang clasped his cane behind his back and walked to the other end of the table. His usual shuffling gait had vanished. He described his meeting with the Arabs. He told them about the three-hundred-million dollar payment, which he characterized as an investment. He omitted that his colleague Dr. Soong, had examined an atomic bomb in Belize. I will lead them to the river, but they must decide to drink. When he stopped speaking, you could hear a pin drop.

A man sitting at the other end of table stood up. "Comrade Chang, why did you delay telling us about this...this most serious matter?" The murmurs indicated that everyone agreed with the man's admonishment. They all stared at Chang waiting for his answer.

"At the time, I wasn't convinced the Arab plot was bona fide. I thought I was the target of a kidnapping plot."

"But we should have been informed."

"And what would you have done?" Chang challenged.

Another member intervened. "Do you know the location and the date of the attack?" Eyebrows were raised in expectation.

"New York City could be the target. I don't know the exact date—at least, not yet."

"But...but, can you obtain the information?" The man stuttering was wide-eyed. The listeners remained silent gazing into their private thoughts.

"It depends," said Chang.

"On?"

"Paying the conspirators the three-hundred million," Chang stated.

"Did he say three-hundred million?" someone asked.

"Why that's preposterous. We must notify the Americans at once," said Wong.

"After a thorough investigation, the Central Intelligence Agency ruled it was an attempted swindle."

"But why don't you believe the CIA?" a guest asked.

"I believe the CIA bungled the investigation. It wouldn't be the first time."

Dr. Wong emerged from his trance taking in the details of what Chang was saying. He stood up, hooked his chubby fingers under his lapels and puffed himself up. He looked like schoolteacher preparing to chastise a student.

"It would seem our esteemed host, Mr. Chang, has been hoodwinked. We all grow old, even you, comrade." Wong shook his head. "Obviously, there was never a threat. Unlike Mr. Chang, I believe the Americans. This was nothing more than an attempt to cheat a rich man in his declining years." Wong sat down with a self-assured smirk locked on his inebriated face.

If looks could kill, Chang's glare would have dropped Wong on the spot.

A guest chastised Wong for his impertinence, but Wong ignored him.

Chang said, "Older and wiser voices can help you find the truth, but only if you are willing to listen. Of course, I say this as a man in his declining years."

They all heckled Wong, who appeared unfazed by the assault.

Chang had set his trap. Wong had obliged him by taking the bait. Chang continued, "Just for argument's sake, let's imagine that these Arabs do, in fact, possess an atomic device and that they intend to detonate the bomb someplace in the United States. Would anyone care to tell us how the world's financial markets would react?"

"A devastating blow of unequalled severity," someone stated. Concerned stares and slow nods indicated that everyone agreed.

Chang described a ripple effect that would paralyze economic activity. He went on to say the sovereign funds could lose as much as five-hundred-billion dollars and that more losses would undoubtedly follow. He ended by mentioning that civil unrest could lead to an overall rebellion. His guests looked very alarmed.

"Mr. Chang, what's the purpose of your fear mongering. There is no bomb," said Wong.

"Yes, but if there were a bomb, shouldn't we act to protect this country?" the same man asked. "Protecting this country's vital interests is our sacred duty."

"And if it meant acting alone, to the detriment of other countries?" Chang asked.

"So be it," Wong said. All heads nodded soberly.

The stage was set. It was time for Chang to describe his plan for advancing China's destiny. The first part of his presentation was based on reducing the sovereign funds' American exposure. The second part called for complicated hedging and arbitrage strategies. The third part instituted the use of derivatives. This would not only insulate the funds, but had the potential of making billions.

Chang sat down and waited for someone to respond. Dr. Wong raised his hand requesting the floor again. "Mr. Chang, I'm sure everyone's impressed by your extensive expertise in financial matters. Maybe you can enlighten us. I ask you once more, what's the purpose of your counterfactual fantasy?"

"I defer to the acclaimed nuclear scientist, Dr. Ming Soong," Chang said.

Dr. Soong stood up and began to speak in terms only other physicists could understand. He was a small bookish man with yellowed teeth and a gravelly voice earned from a lifetime of heavy smoking. No one in China knew more about nuclear energy. It wasn't often that he was given the opportunity to lecture such important men about his life's work; he was determined to make the most of it. He droned on for ten minutes without direction. His listeners squirmed.

Mercifully, Chang interceded. "Dr. Soong, please fast forward. Tell them what you discovered on the cargo ship in Belize."

This time, Soong used concise language. There was no misunderstanding. He had examined a nuclear weapon on an island freighter in Central America. When he finished speaking, the audience was hushed for what seemed like an eternity.

An inebriated guest didn't hear Soong. He slurped his soup so loudly it sounded like a chainsaw at a funeral. Chang grabbed the man's spoon. The men at the table glared at the transgressor. He grinned lopsidedly.

"Thank you, Dr. Soong. You may sit down. Comments?"

"Assuming New York City is the target, does the doctor have a casualty estimate?"

Dr. Song took the floor again. "Using Nagasaki as a model and with a bomb of this magnitude and with such a concentrated population, I would put the death count at around 500,000 plus or minus." There were groans and gasps and hand-wringing.

"What about the economic damage?"

"Beyond comprehension," declared an attendee.

"Losses will be in the trillions."

"America buys forty percent of our exports," someone interjected.

"How will they repay their loans? Everything we've achieved will be lost."

The men at the table were too traumatized to speak. Collective trepidation filled their faces.

Chang got up, walked over and stood behind Dr. Wong. He put his cane on Wong's shoulder. Wong scooped up a rice-ball with his chopsticks, but he couldn't eat it. His face was fatigued. He slumped forward in a dejected slouch.

"Dr. Wong, you and I have crossed swords many times, but I have never doubted your undying patriotism. We find ourselves as stewards of our country's fate. We didn't ask for it, but here we are. Historians will etch our epitaphs. Let them write that we stood united to insure our country's destiny."

Chang sat down. Dr Wong rose slowly and faced Chang. His eyes remained downcast. "I hope you will accept my apology, comrade. One is reminded of the ancient proverb, 'A rat who gnaws on a cat's tail invites destruction.'" Even Chang was amused.

Wong raised his hands to quiet them. His sagging shoulders indicated defeat. "I make a motion that we adopt Comrade Chang's strategy for protecting the sovereign funds."

Dr. Soong seconded the motion.

"Are there any dissenters?" a man asked.

There were none.

The meeting was adjourned.

24

Jesse requested an audience with Gordon Wells. At that meeting, he was saddened to see Gordon's deterioration. He seemed listless. His eyes were cloudy. Sean was especially disappointed to learn that Laura had returned to Washington. After Sean completed his account of his get-together with Robert Barrett and the subsequent call he received, Gordon Wells muttered a barrage of obscenities. "This isn't at all what I expected."

"So, where do we go from here?" Jesse said.

Wells thought for a moment. He fished a bottle of pills from his breast pocket and handed them to Sean. "Well, the first thing I need to do is to stop taking these. I can't think when I'm flying as high as a kite. Speaking about flying, Jesse, I've got a job for you."

Gordon explained that after 9/11, the Federal Aviation Authority recorded all international flights at the FAA headquarters in Oklahoma City. Jesse's mission was to use his government credentials to obtain the registration number of Chang's private jet. His next assignment was to find out if the aircraft had made any recent international flights.

Gordon said, "In my opinion, the jury's still out. We're missing something. What that something is, I haven't a clue. If it is real, Chang wouldn't give those Arabs a dime without personally inspecting the weapon. You can bet he'd use his private airplane to fly someplace in the world to examine it.

"Wouldn't he just send someone?"

"Chang doesn't trust anyone. No, he'd make that trip in person. Of course, this is all very hypothetical."

Sean said to Gordon, "You have to admit, the evidence *is* becoming more compelling."

"I'd say the evidence is more confusing than compelling."

Gordon asked Rigby, "Any sign of the men who confronted you at the marina?"

"Neither hide nor hair."

"Mr. Croxford, your job's to find out as much as you can about Luther James's death. I'd start by going back to the bar where you met him. I think that just about covers everything."

Sean said, "Isn't there something I can do?"

Instead of answering, Gordon said, "Gentlemen, I'd like to speak to Mr. Mahoney in private."

Rigby and Jesse excused themselves. The atmosphere had become tense.

Sean spoke before Gordon could. "I know what this is about."

"Do you, now." Gordon looked disappointed having been cheated out of his scolding. "Let's hear it."

"Are my intentions concerning your daughter honorable?"

"Come now, Mr. Mahoney, I was born at night, but not last night. Men's intentions are seldom honorable when it concerns women. Laura's happiness means everything to me. You hurt her, and for that, I cannot forgive. In a way, I feel responsible for you two getting together.

Sean thought for a moment before answering. He picked his words carefully. "You daughter's an amazing woman. Look, I'm no bargain, but if I let her get away, I know I'll regret it for the rest of my life. Am I making any sense?"

The silence was awkward as Gordon weighed his response. "We make two or three key decisions during our lives. I'm not sure you're interested in hearing mine, but here goes. I offer no apologies for my life, only the nagging fear of my daughter's disappointment. I..."

Sean cut in. "Your daughter says you're the kindest man she's ever known and the smartest. No man can ask for a better legacy."

Gordon shrugged his shoulders. He appeared overcome. "Sean, you've hijacked my thunder." He thought for a few seconds and then he asked, "How did your divorce play out?"

Sean told him about hiring Carmine and the events culminating with the scene in Morris Ackerman's office. As he spoke he watched the distaste in Gordon's eyes dissipate. When he finished, Gordon laughed. "One is reminded of Homer. 'Revenge is far sweeter than flowing honey.'"

"I'd like to contact your daughter, if I have your permission."

Gordon removed his glasses. "If I'm any judge of character, and I think that I am, I'd say you've redeemed yourself, at least in my eyes. Why not talk to her in person. She's on the five o'clock flight from Miami."

Sean looked relieved. "Gordon, I'll do the right thing by Laura. You have my word on it."

"That's all I ask. As I said, I'm afraid my days here on earth are drawing to an end. I'm willing to leave this world, but only after I know my daughter's ship has been righted. Before you go, I have an unrelated question. Those photographs you told me about. You said your producer has one set. Are there any other sets floating around? Again, I'm not passing judgment."

Sean's expression spelled embarrassment. "I really can't say."

"For the life of me, I don't know why Chang used them to get you fired. There were other ways of getting that documentary canceled or at least getting it delayed."

"I thought Chang liked me."

Gordon opened his hands. "Chang doesn't like people, pure and simple. The devil works in malicious ways. Goodnight, Sean. And good luck tomorrow."

After Gordon was alone, he typed the following email to a friend at Scotland Yard in London:

Dear Philip,

Re: Nelson Chang, aka Nelson Bridges.
Were you able to resurrect the file on the unsolved murder case: Mr. and Mrs. Robert Bridges of Manchester, UK? More specifically, was their adopted son ever a suspect?

Best Regards,
Gordon

The following reply flashed on his computer screen:

Dear Gordon,

Re: Murder investigation.
The Bridges died from ingesting Tetrodotoxin,
a rare poison extracted from fugu puffer-fish
found only in the Far East. Port wine was found
in the victims' stomachs. As such, it was
concluded that the wine was the delivery
method. The bottle containing the poison was
never found. The in-house toxicologist stated
that the perpetrator must have hated the
Bridges. The victims died slow painful deaths.
Nelson Chang, at that time known as Nelson
Bridges, was out of the country and was
therefore never a suspect.

It should also be noted that the Bridges's two
biological sons died six months earlier in a
boating accident. Their adopted son, Nelson
survived the incident. Your speculation was
well-founded; Chang was the Bridges's sole
heir.

Cheers,
Philip

Gordon let the details of the case move through his
mind. He realized there was a possibility that Nelson
Chang had not only murdered his adoptive parents, but
his two stepbrothers as well. In fairness, Scotland Yard

had no way of knowing what kind of a man Chang would become. If they had, their investigation might have taken a different turn. What kind of a monster kills his parents, he asked himself. Was Chang capable of helping jihadists attack the United States? The answer made the hair on the back of his neck stand up.

25

Rigby ordered a whiskey neat at Cracker Jack's. Jesse ordered a rum and coke. The bartender stopped cleaning his fingernails with a knife and quartered a lime with it. What teeth he had were brown. Jesse yelled, "Eighty-six the lime, please." After holding the glass up to the light, Jesse used his handkerchief to clean its rim. Lil was posted up on her usual perch at the other end of the bar. The vestiges of her black eye were still visible. She was thinner than Rigby had remembered her. Lil's wrinkled face was the color of a dried apricot. Jesse tried to engage her in conversation, but she acted aloof.

And then, out of the blue, she whispered, "Psst, I can't be with ya'll." Lil's blackened tooth had dropped out. The gap made trilling sounds when she spoke.

"Pardon me?" Rigby said.

"Ya see—I have a new boyfriend."

"Sorry to hear about your loss, I mean about Luther."

"Yeah, well, shit happens." She appeared irritated by his empathy.

The bartender seemed interested in their conversation and moved within earshot.

"Any idea about who killed Luther," said Jesse.

"Say feller, you ain't from around here." Lil said this to Rigby, ignoring Jesse.

Rigby shook his head. Lil continued. "Your friend ain't much of a talker, is he? Truth is—I'm livin' with Luther's brother, Delbert. He don't like me talkin' to strangers."

She got the bartender's attention and said something under her breath. The bartender motioned to the men playing pool. They suspended their game and moved closer. The largest man was almost a giant. He stroked a pool cue. Some of his teeth were rotten. He wore dirty rubber boots and a greasy t-shirt with a Confederate flag inscribed on the back.

Rigby drained his whiskey and slid the glass forward. "Could my friend get a clean glass this time?"

"There ain't gonna be a 'this time.' I think you two, better *get*," the barkeep said.

"Lighten up, friend. What's your problem?" Rigby's nervy tone unsettled him.

"The problem's with him." The bartender nodded at Jesse. "Know why coloreds wear hats, don't ya?" When he didn't get a response, he said, "So the birds don't shit on their lips. Get it?"

Rigby didn't laugh. Jesse stood up and turned until he was back-to-back with Rigby.

"We don't get many jiggaboos around these parts. Sorry, I meant to say Americans of an African persuasion." His snickering was contagious. The pool players giggled like teenage girls. Their faces flushed by whiskey, turned even redder.

Jesse said, "Know how to circumcise a redneck?"

"No, I can't say that I do," replied the man behind the bar.

"You kick his sister in the jaw."

"Hey, that ain't funny," roared the giant. He rested the cue on his shoulder.

"I think we've seen the last of you two peckerheads," said the bartender.

Rigby used a bad southern imitation. "Uh-oh, now you've gone and done it. You hurt my friend's feelings. He don't take kindly to ignoramuses. Lil, you best call for two ambulances."

Lil's smoker's cough prevented an answer. She cleared her throat and croaked, "Why two ambulances?"

"Jesse, think two is enough?" Rigby asked.

That got a smile from Jesse. "Two should do just fine."

The pool players' faces were marked by deep thinking as they mulled over the need for two ambulances. Another moment of excruciating silence passed as Jesse and Rigby waited for a reaction.

"God damn, I reckon you boys want this the hard way." The bartender sighed and retrieved a Louisville slugger from underneath the cash register.

"We didn't come here looking for trouble," Jesse said.

"I'd say you boys're in a heap of shit." The barkeep smirked. He grabbed Rigby's wrist, but before he could swing the baseball bat, Rigby smashed him in the face with his beer mug. The tobacco plug behind his lower lip popped out with a tooth. Jesse jerked the baseball bat free and struck the closest assailant knocking him to the floor. He swirled and hit the next one, also knocking him down. The big man holding the pool cue stepped back out of range.

"What's your pleasure, friend?" Rigby said inching forward. The man slid his hands down the small end of the cue. As he drew back the unwieldy stick, Rigby whirled and back-kicked him. His heel found its mark. The big man clutched his privates and fell to his knees. He gagged, spit, and wiped his mouth. Jesse reached down and pulled the Smith and Wesson from its ankle holster. He pressed the barrel into the man's ear. "Are you gonna make me shoot you?" The man shook his head.

"Barkeep, we'll have those drinks," Rigby said.

The bartender checked his mouth for blood. "You son of a bitch, you busted my fuckin' jaw."

Rigby disregarded him and turned to Lil who was biting her balled-up fist like a frightened child. She panted. "Lord knows, I like my men on the rough side."

Jesse said, "Ma'am, we need to know what happened to Luther."

"Damn fool got himself killed."

"Who killed him?"

"Why, fuck, it coulda been anyone of a hunnert. Luther had a shit-load of enemies and I mean a shit-load. I didn't hate him none, but I didn't cry when I heard he was dead. That's all I know."

"Fair enough," said Jesse.

Lil tossed back her hair and announced breathlessly, "Delbert's on a fishin' trip, if either of you is interested." She pouted and ruffled her blouse enough to show sagging cleavage.

"Better call for those ambulances, Lil." Rigby tossed some money on the bar and walked out. Jesse backed out behind him.

As they were getting into their car, Jesse said, "I could wait in the car if you have designs on Lil."

"Me? You're the one she wanted," Rigby said.

Jesse grimaced. "Not if she was the last woman in the world."

"Why, I bet old Lil's got some hidden talents."

"Oh, really. One thing's for sure, grieving ain't one of them,"

"A man needs a sense of adventure in life," Rigby said grinning. "That's the trouble with you, Jesse. No sense of adventure."

"Croxford, having you for a friend is about all the adventure one man can stand. Can I ask you a question?"

"Sure."

"How come you didn't hit the big one first?"

"Past experience, old boy. The lion who roars is seldom the lion that kills."

"Wow, I just learned something."

"There's a lot I can teach you, Jesse."

"Let's not get carried away."

The Key West mortuary was located on Truman Avenue. It's a concrete building tucked between two weather-beaten clapboard houses. The sign out front read: $1200 Cremation. Package includes removal, transportation, storage, casket rental and viewing.

A heavyset man with greasy hair answered the door. His eyes looked in opposite directions. He swallowed a mouthful of food and announced, "Sorry, sports fans, we're closed." The man glanced nervously at the pornographic magazine on his desk. He reached down and checked his zipper.

"Did the Sherriff call you about us?" Jesse said.

[167]

"No one called me about nothin'. I was eatin' my…"

"Did you know there's a state statute prohibiting the display of sexual material on the premises of a funeral home?" Jesse pointed at the magazine.

"Hey man, nobody ever told me that." He looked like a person unfettered by profound thoughts. He seemed more perplexed than embarrassed.

"Did you hear that, Mr. Croxford? No one ever told him. What's your name, son?"

Rigby shook his head in amazement.

"Kevin Casey."

"Casey with a C?" said Jesse.

"That's right. Am I in trouble? Why hell, I'm just the night watchman here. Did you say you're with the Monroe County sheriff's department?"

Instead of answering, Jesse opened his wallet and showed him his ATF identity card. Before Kevin could read it, he snapped the wallet shut.

Jesse said, "Don't worry. We're all brothers in law enforcement. Isn't that right, Mr. Croxford?" Rigby tried unsuccessfully to stop smiling.

Kevin squeezed an angry pimple on his neck. "I've had a job application in with the sheriff for now on three years. Maybe you could put a good word in for me?"

"Let me think about that one. Back to business. We're here to view the remains of a Luther James."

When Rigby pretended to grab a piece of fried fish from Kevin's plate, he looked panic-stricken. He encircled the plate with his arms and growled.

"Where's the cooler?" Jesse asked.

Kevin stuffed the dirty magazine under a newspaper. "The bodies are kept in the backroom."

The dead room had metal lockers on the walls and a stainless steel autopsy table in the middle. The floor and the ceiling were covered by white ceramic tile. A flowery disinfectant veiled embalming fluid.

"James, James," Kevin said reading the names. "Here we go. Say hello to Mr. Luther James." He pulled out the gurney and stepped back with a grin locked on his pimply face.

Jesse unzipped the plastic body bag. Luther James's corpse was headless. The white tracheal and esophageal stumps looked like cannelloni tubes caked in marinara sauce.

"The county coroner had to identify him by his tats." Kevin pulled up his collar.

Luther's chest tattoo was a human skull sprouting wings. The words beneath the tattoo had been removed by acid or burning. He had swastikas on both biceps and spider webs on his elbows. Rigor mortis wrinkling made the smaller inscriptions unreadable.

"Brrr. Wonder what happened to his head?" Rigby rubbed his hands together.

Kevin hiked his shoulders. "Probably the sharks ate his head." He scratched his lowest chin with one hand and realigned his genitals with the other. A wrinkled brow hinted unaccustomed mental exercise.

Jesse used a ballpoint pen to gingerly peel away the layers of severed flesh letting him inspect the jagged saw-blade marks on what was now a stump. Jesse turned Luther's right hand over. The tattooed letters on his knuckles spelled "weed." The fingernails were blue and cleaner now, having been soaked in saltwater.

[169]

"I think we've seen enough. Thanks, Kevin, you've been helpful."

"No problem. Hey, don't forget to put that word in with the sheriff."

"Consider it done. I'd dump the pornography, if I were you."

"Hey, I swear to God, that magazine ain't mine."

"Better get rid of it anyway."

"You bet I will. And thanks, mister." Kevin tugged his scrotum and closed the door.

26

S ean rehearsed what he would say to Laura as he drove to a florist shop on east Duval Street. He bought a dozen yellow roses.

By the time he arrived at the airport, the passengers from Miami were already disembarking. He saw Laura and shouted, but she couldn't hear him. The man walking beside her grabbed her carry-on. Sean hid behind a concrete pillar. When he saw the man hug Laura and kiss her cheek, he was devastated. As he was leaving the terminal, he started to throw the roses into a trash can, but changed his mind. He handed the flowers to a tourist. "Welcome to Key West,"

"Thank you. What a lovely surprise," the woman said.

Somehow, lovely doesn't work for me today, Sean thought.

The cocktail hour at Gordon's house convened on time. Everyone was delighted to see Gordon's improvement. He seemed more alert and his speech wasn't as slurred. Sean was absent. When Jesse said Sean was ill, Gordon didn't press him on the details. He had intended to speak to his daughter about Sean, but a surprise visitor made it inconvenient.

"What did you find out about Mr. James's death?" Gordon asked Jesse.

Jesse said the sheriff's homicide investigation reported that Luther was killed over a drug deal gone sour. Cutting his head off wasn't meant to hide his identity. Luther had more tattoos than a circus freak. The report stated that decapitation sends a message to rival drug smugglers.

"The welcoming committee at that bar supports the sheriff's claim," Rigby added.

"Perhaps, but Luther's murder could've been made to look drug-related," Gordon said. "His body *was* found in the marina where Sean's yacht is docked."

They looked bewildered. Finally, Jesse said to Gordon, "I thought you said Sean's Arab plot was a fantasy. What changed your mind?"

"Nothing's changed. I'm still ninety percent sure the CIA has it right. If we sit back and do nothing and something does happen—who wants to live with that guilt trip? And some unanswered questions about Mr. Chang have surfaced. Things still don't add up."

Laura had been eavesdropping from the kitchen. She stepped forward and asked. "Can I say something?"

"Please do," her father said.

"Has anyone thought about the date?"

"Which is?"

"In a few days it'll be May second."

"What's so important about that date?" Sean asked.

"Osama Bin Laden was killed on May second."

Her father thought for a moment. "Heightened security makes that date unlikely. Again, I'm speaking theoretically. There's no sense continuing this discussion without Sean. We need his input."

"I'll go get him," Jesse offered.

"No. Laura, you go," Gordon insisted.

Laura found Sean sleeping it off in Harry's Hatteras. She had trouble rousing him. He looked at her sleepy-eyed and muttered, "Oh, it's you. Whatdaya want?" He rubbed his eyes and yawned.

"No it's great to see you or how have you been, Laura? My father sent me. He needs you."

"Can't it wait? As you can see, I'm a little under the weather." He smacked his lips and yawned again. "Besides, your father thinks I'm crazy." He lit a cigarette and blew out the match.

"No, it can't wait. He doesn't think you're crazy. I think you're crazy." She picked up a half-empty glass, sniffed the contents and faked a gag.

Sean changed the subject. "What about him?"

"What about who?" she replied.

"The man I saw you with at the airport yesterday."

"Careful sailor, you're in dangerous waters. Better come hard over. Besides, what's that gotta do with you?"

"It has everything to do with me," he replied.

She raised an eyebrow and chewed on her lower lip. "Hmm. What about what's-her-name?"

"Ancient history. I'm officially divorced."

Laura's green eyes narrowed as she waited for the details.

"Oh, really." she said.

"Yes, really. Are you in love with this creep?"

"Sure, I love Tyler. And he's not a creep."

"You never mentioned anyone by that name."

"You weren't listening."

Sean blinked from the smoke. "Oh no, you didn't. I would have remembered that name."

She looked more amused than irritated. "You're such an idiot. Get dressed."

He leaned back and exhaled more smoke. "Not before you tell me about lover-boy."

"Sean, Tyler's my brother. That's why I flew to Washington. I was determined to see my father and my brother reunited before, well, you know. He flew home this afternoon."

Sean paused momentarily shaking his head. "You're right, I *am* an idiot." He thumped his forehead with his knuckles.

His expression turned serious. "Laura, certain foods give me gas and sometimes I forget to put the toilet seat down and I'm told I snore. What I'm trying to say is, I'm not for everyone, but I know I can make you happy."

"Wow, what a lovely proposal." In spite of her best efforts, she failed to hide her pleasure.

"You know what they say? Honesty's the best path to a healthy marriage," Sean said.

"Whoever said that's an asshole. Better yet, make that a divorced asshole," she said.

Sean let the injured look fall from his face. He finger-combed his hair back and asked, "Well, whatdaya say?"

"If you do something about the gas, I'm all in." She subdued a grin. "And quit smoking."

"Hey, don't get carried away," he said. "Any other demands?"

"Get dressed. And put out that cigarette."

"Did anyone ever call you a domineering bitch?"

"Only one."

"Let me guess. The guy you dumped."

"Yup."

One hour later, the meeting was reconvened in Gordon's orchid house. Gordon noted the change in his daughter. He caught a glimpse of Sean and his daughter locking eyes. He was elated and it showed.

"Now, that we're all accounted for—Jesse, why don't you tell us what you found out."

Jesse told them that Nelson Chang's private jet was registered to a corporation domiciled in the Isle of Man. The aircraft made a recent international flight from Hong Kong to Belize with a brief stopover in San Francisco. The passenger manifest included a Sudanese national and the Chinese nuclear physicist, Dr. Ming Soong. Mentioning a nuclear physicist got their interest.

"Let's not get carried away," Gordon warned. "China's constructing nuclear power plants in the Caribbean."

Jesse continued by telling them that Chang's Gulfstream spent two days on the ramp at the Belize International Airport before returning to Hong Kong with a refueling stop in Seattle. When queried about Chang's activities in Belize, Jesse said Chang was accompanied by a military escort to a seaside resort located on the coast.

"Was there anything else?" Gordon asked Jesse.

"A friend of mine, who works for the DEA, showed me a list of the ships currently operating in the Caribbean. One freighter caught my eye. The Caribbean Moon is anchored at the same resort where Chang and his friends stayed.

"I don't see the connection."

"Get this—the ship's registered to a company in Yemen."

"So, what's your point?" Gordon asked.

"That transporting an atomic weapon in a cargo container makes sense. You have to admit, it is a possibility."

"My God, are you seriously suggesting..." Gordon thought about it momentarily and then he said, "I suppose, anything's possible. We're pissing in the wind, please excuse my French. We need to end this once and for all. Sean, you and Laura fly to New York. Tell this agent Barrett you'd like an audience with his supervisor. Laura, tell them you're Sean's attorney and that you're considering legal action because Sean lost his job. Be sure to tell them you're my daughter. Threaten subpoenas. In other words, wing it. See what kind of a response you get."

Gordon glanced at his daughter nervously.

"Jesse, you and Rigby fly down to Belize. Do some snooping. Bribe some people. Jesse, maybe you can use your ATF credentials to get onboard that ship and inspect the cargo. I'm betting you won't find anything. At least it'll satisfy your creative imaginations."

He grabbed Laura's hand and held it against his cheek.

"I'll hold down the fort. We meet back here in three days. We can celebrate the end of this lunacy. Get on with our lives, so to speak." Gordon smiled.

"And if we find a bomb on that ship. Then what happens?" Jesse asked.

"The only thing you'll find is a few rattraps." In spite of his best effort to hide it, Gordon's eyes implied uneasiness. "If we're all in agreement, I move we call it a night."

The following night an epiphany came to Gordon Wells in a dream. He sat up in bed and thought, Wick Harrington, you magnificent bastard. This is your doing. How could I have been so stupid? Has to be the vicodin. He struggled from the bed into his wheelchair.

He typed the following email messages on his laptop:

> Dear Laura,
>
> Hallelujah! I've seen the light. Can't believe it took me so long. There is no threat. Never was. Very complicated. Fill you in on the details when I see you. Hurry home.
> Love,
> Your father
>
> Dear Jesse,
> Hope you receive this in time. There is no threat. Do not, I repeat, do not speak to anyone about this before I brief you. I know everything. Very complicated.
> Fill you in on the details when you get here.
>
> Best regards,
> Gordon

He maneuvered his wheelchair down the wooden ramp connected to the hothouse. As the incline leveled, his eyes adjusted to the incandescent lighting. White orchids now looked bluish. Irrigation misting made the muggy air unbreatheable. He was checking the nutrient-flow timers when the downpour started. Driving rain cloaked the sound of hissing sprinklers. Rumbling thunder rattled the overhead glass panels. A snake of jagged lightning startled him. The lights flickered twice before going out.

He rolled his way back to the bottom of the ramp in the dark. A thunder clap masked the sound of breaking glass. He felt the temperature drop and knew the hothouse had been violated. Lightning illuminated a huge man silhouetted in the doorway. "You there, what do you want?"

The man didn't move a muscle.

"There's money on the nightstand in my bedroom. Take what you want and leave me in peace."

The man didn't answer or budge.

"Who are you?" Gordon sounded shriller this time. At that moment, he knew it wasn't a robbery.

The man came at him slowly. His footsteps made sloshing sounds. Gordon's voice was more composed now. "You think I'm afraid of you? Go fuck yourself."

The intruder slipped a hangman's noose over Gordon's head and yanked it taut. Gordon gulped his final breath of air. The man tossed the other end of the rope over a steel girder and heaved until Gordon's emaciated body was vaulted into the rafters. He writhed and wiggled as his bare feet searched desperately for the floor. Within seconds, the struggling subsided. He dangled motionless, but his brain was still alive. Time slowed down into a dreamlike unreality. A kaleidoscope of memories flashed in his mind until there was only a vision of his daughter. The bright light faded into darkness. Gordon Wells died.

The killer moved closer to examine the body. A stroke of lightning revealed bulging lifeless eyes. Satisfied, the killer left the greenhouse and disappeared into the storm.

JAMES GARDNER

27

Belize
April 25

Bribes are as routine as night following day in Belize. As an ATF agent, Jesse Spooner had excellent police contacts, but greasing palms was more expedient. One hour after their arrival in Belize City, they knew Nelson Chang's itinerary. They even hired the same limousine, absent the military escort. Three hours later they checked into the same seaside resort.

The Caribbean Moon was still anchored offshore. Jesse said the on-deck activity was proof that the freighter was preparing to get underway. Scuttlebutt at the resort confirmed his opinion; the ship was set to weigh anchor on the next high tide. The ship's final destination was the Port of Miami.

Later that night, Rigby said, "If we're gonna get a look at that ship's cargo—I suggest we do it now."

"Looks like a long way. You know, I'm not much of a swimmer." Jesse stared at the freighter. "How far is it?"

"Three hundred meters, give or take. I wouldn't worry about drowning. Why hell, the sharks'll eat us before we get halfway." Rigby grinned.

"I didn't see any sharks today." Jesse's Adam's apple lodged midway in his throat.

"Sharks are night-feeders."

"Great. Why do I let you talk me into this shit?" Jesse shook his head.

"Some men are born to lead and others are...well, you know."

"Don't go there, Croxford."

The Caribbean Moon rolled gently from the light inshore breeze. The monotonous drone of her generator carried on the water. Wispy clouds screened a crescent moon. Waves lapping on the beach made whooshing sounds.

"This is fuckin' crazy," Jesse whispered.

"Shhh!" Rigby put his hand over Jesse's mouth. They hid behind a coconut palm waiting for a cloud to hide the moonshine. When it did, they ran down the beach and waded in up to their necks. Halfway to the ship, Jesse sputtered, "I'll never make it."

"Relax, God damn it." Rigby placed his arm over Jesse's chest and started frog-kicking. It was slow-going, but they made it. Jesse clung to a rope-ladder as Rigby climbed up over the gunnels. He reached down and pulled Jesse up onto the deck. Jesse tried to whisper, but Rigby shushed him again. The freighter was unlit. They crept forward to the stacked cargo containers. The first container had been left unlocked. Rigby slid the latch over. Jesse swung the door open and froze. They heard voices coming from the bowels of the ship. Two men climbed up out of the cargo hold. Rigby and Jesse stayed in the shadows until the deckhands' voices disappeared into the pilothouse.

"Let's get the fuck outta here," Jesse said.

They were over the side in a flash. The swim in was easier. A floodlight turned night into day, its beam probing the darkness, sweeping past them and then returning.

"*Alto!*" The command was magnified by a megaphone. Two armed men walked out of the shadows.

"*Pongan las manos!*"

Jesse and Rigby dog-paddled to shallower water and then waded ashore.

"Easy, *amigos*," said Jesse, squinting from the light. "We're guests in the hotel."

Jesse dropped his hands. Rigby also lowered his hands. The guards motioned them back up with their guns. A guard spoke in broken English. "*Senor*, the beach it is closed *de noche.*"

Rigby and Jesse were escorted back to their villa. The hotel manager joined them. He was an unremarkable looking man had it not been for his buck teeth. Jesse presented his ATF credentials. The manager apologized, but explained that tourists had been robbed on the beach at night. It was recommended that guests stay in their rooms after dark.

The following morning, Jesse looked out of his window and breathed a huge sigh of relief. The Caribbean Moon had weighed anchor during the night. "Phew. Thank God. I had a nightmare about trying to make that swim again."

"Jesse, you're no Michael Phelps."

"I told you I couldn't swim worth a shit. You know something, Croxford. You really are, certifiably insane."

"Me? You went along with it. Now who's crazy?"

"I would've loved getting a look at those containers. No security tells me we were sent on a wild goose chase," Jesse said.

Rigby didn't answer.

28

New York City
April 26

After reading Gordon's text message, Sean called Robert Barrett and canceled their meeting. Sean apologized for his hysteria and added that he now accepted the CIA's interpretation of his Hong Kong experience. As far as he was concerned, the matter was closed. Barrett absolved him of blame by reiterating the importance of vigilant citizens coming forward. Their conversation ended on a positive note.

At the same time Rigby and Jesse boarded their flight for Miami, Sean and Laura were sound asleep in Sean's apartment. They silenced their cell phones for an obvious reason. Laura missed the incoming call from the Monroe County sheriff's department. Sean didn't receive a call from the last person in the world he wanted to talk to.

Sean woke up first. He was ordering their breakfast delivered in, when he had an incoming call. "Good morning, darling," said his ex-wife.

"Never expected to hear from you," he whispered.

"Can I come up?" she asked.

Sean shook his head even though he was talking on a telephone. "This isn't a good time." He whispered inaudibly, but Laura knew he was talking to his ex-wife.

"Is someone with you?"

His answer was as indefinite as he could make it. "Yes, you could say that."

"Sure didn't take you long." She paused and then she added, "I had no right to say that."

"Go on. Get to the point."

"We need to talk," she said.

Laura sat up in bed. Sean shrugged apologetically. Laura shook her head.

"Where are you?"

"The coffee shop on 59th."

"Stay put. I'm there in ten minutes."

He hung up and said to Laura, "Get dressed, you're coming with me."

"No way. I'm not interested in being compared to "Miss America" this early in the morning. You're on your own, kiddo." She rolled over and pulled the blanket over her head.

It was a fifteen-minute walk from his apartment, just enough time to clear his mind, but when he saw her his heart raced. She was sitting at a window table. Everyone stared at her and then him. He knew they were thinking, what's with this middle-aged geezer and this gorgeous babe. According to Kathy, Copernicus was wrong; she's the center of the universe. Sean smiled to himself. She glanced up at him and smiled back. He felt his heart flutter. She stood up and presented her cheek, which he kissed. Her smell reddened his cheeks.

"You look spectacular," he said. "But then you always look great."

"What does she look like?" she asked disregarding his compliment.

"Who?" He looked uncomfortable.

She studied her fingernails. "The woman in our apartment, that's who."

"It's not our apartment, it's my apartment. If you don't believe me, just ask your boyfriend-slash-lawyer."

"Is she better looking than, say, I am?" she asked ignoring the insult. She batted her eyes and pursed her lips together. Her faultless face, immobilized by fillers, was hard to read.

Sean tried more flattery, but this time he attached sarcasm. "Kathy, you're the best-looking woman in this city, but then you already know that."

Again she overlooked the denigrating footnote. "Guess there's no chance of us getting back together."

"My God, you can't be serious. Not after what we've been through. Our marriage was one of convenience. It didn't start out that way, at least not for me, but that's the way it ended. Let's remember the good times and move on with our lives."

"What's she like?" she asked, not listening to a word he said. She looked past him admiring herself from different angles in the window's reflection.

"Laura's special. You wouldn't understand." At that moment, he felt sorry for his ex-wife.

"Oh, I get it. The woman's a saint. Well, fuck you *and* your girlfriend." She said this loud enough to draw glances from the people sitting at the other tables. The men looked puzzled. It was like they were asking themselves, why would he dump her for another one?

"What do you want from me?" Sean asked.

She looked away. The impasse ended with her saying, "He used me. I know that now." She blotted make-believe tears with a hanky.

"Ackerman?" Sean said this more for himself than her.

She waited a long time before acknowledging him with a tearful nod.

"Kathy, you always deserved better."

"Don't patronize me." She thought for several moments. Finally, she said, "He's out to get you. I told him you'd never use those photographs. He doesn't believe me."

"Screw him and his elevator shoes."

"He really is revolting, isn't he?" She giggled nervously. Distaste puckered her perfect lips.

"Ackerman's no George Clooney."

"I'm involved with someone else. He's in modeling." She looked vague. He knew his ex-wife was lying. "Sweetheart, you can have any man in this city. Just be careful, you have no talent for poverty."

"I can have any man in this city but the one I want." This time her tears were real.

Sean tried to shore up her self-esteem. "My time with you was the best part of my life."

She took a long sip of coffee giving her time to think. Her eyes revealed she knew reconciliation was out of the question. She brushed a few loose hair strands behind her ear and looked into his eyes. "Be careful, Sean. Ackerman's a vindictive little bastard. I know more than I can say."

"Don't worry about me. Worry about yourself."

"I won't bother you again," she said. "I promise."

"Nonsense. I'll always be there for you." It was one of those acceptable lies people tell to ease the tension of ending a relationship. He kissed his ex-wife goodbye and left her. He never looked back.

The sky outside was darkening with clouds that hinted rain. A couple of times he broke into a zigzagging jog. Wary New York pedestrians gave way. He bypassed the elevator and bounded up the three flights of stairs. Laura was taking a shower. He slipped out of his clothes and joined her. They held each other for a long time. There wasn't a need to speak. Laura knew she was the only woman in Sean's life.

29

Hong Kong
April 27

The jihadists requested an audience with Nelson Chang. The emergency meeting took place on April 27 onboard the Honeyguide. The attendance was the same as it had been when they revealed their fatwa. At that meeting, they demanded a one-hundred-million dollar advance. Chang opposed the request by citing the possibility of unforeseen obstacles. The Arabs argued forcefully, but in the end they agreed to Chang's proviso. The three hundred million would be electronically transferred immediately after the detonation.

The exact time and date of the attack came as no surprise. It would take place on the second of May commemorating the death of Osama Bin Laden.

General Obon hid behind his expensive sunglasses and remained quiet. His yawning and head bobs indicated that he'd had a rough night. His co-conspirators eyed him with contempt.

Chang had assumed that New York City would be the target. But the conspirators rejected New York because of heightened security. Newly installed radiation screening portals in and around New York's harbor entrances were sensitive enough to detect a tooth x-ray. The likelihood of a ship's transporting atomic material and getting close to the city was improbable. Instead, they selected Miami as ground zero. Miami-Dade County was the eighth most populated area in the United States. Three million people lived inside of the target zone. Prevailing southeast winds would blow the radiation cloud north into heavily populated coastal towns.

The plan called for the Caribbean Moon to penetrate U.S. territorial waters on Saturday morning. The freighter would dock at the Port of Miami. The cargo container concealing the nuclear device would be offloaded and stacked with hundreds of other containers awaiting overland shipment by rail and trucks. No cargo inspections were scheduled on weekends. Detonation would take place on Monday morning. To test the port's security, the terrorists shipped radioactive material in five separate cargo containers from five different locations in Central America. All of the cargo containers entered the port undetected.

As Chang listened, he accepted the inevitability of the attack. Failing health and a desire to advance China's agenda overcame his accustomed skepticism. Chang closed his eye pretending to listen to his co-conspirators discuss the attack's aftermath. He was thinking about the biopsy of blame. The perpetrators will be exposed within hours. I have evidence showing that I warned the Americans. I have the recording of my conversation with

China's double agent, Ho Leng. CIA won't admit to the blunder. Their obsession for secrecy is my protection.

Chang had received a coded communiqué from Ho Leng, his mole working at the CIA. Hidden in her industrial drivel were two important facts. Leng believed the atomic device in question was no longer in Russian hands. Secondly, Sean Mahoney and his brother-in-law had contacted the same CIA agent in New York. Chang viewed the first fact favorably. It affirmed his judgment that the jihadists' plot was authentic. The second fact was troubling. The final stages of his financial terrorism were about to be implemented. The last thing he wanted was to have the attack foiled at the last minute.

30

The Caribbean Moon entered the Florida Straits on April 28 at 0400 hours. The freighter cleared the eastern tip of Cuba around midnight and was now on a 280 degree heading. She was making twelve knots. The Gulfstream current would increase her speed to fifteen knots when she turned on a more northerly course. Distant lights twinkled in Cuba's Sierra Mountains. Phosphorous plankton made the ship's boiling wake iridescent. The Cuban gunboats that had shadowed her were gone. Probably headed back to Havana, the captain thought. He checked the radar screen. Three ships traveling in the opposite direction were spread out to her portside. A ship on the same heading was behind him. Things were as they should be. It was clear sailing all the way to Miami.

"Come right sixty degrees to three-four-zero."
"Aye aye, captain," said the man on watch.

The old ship creaked and moaned as she came about in the heavy swells.

One hour later, the morning was still part of the night, but its color was turning gray in the east. Flying fish on transparent wings skipped away from the ship's bow like flat stones hurled against a pond. Her wake had lost its glow with the approach of sunrise.

As the captain checked the ship's position, he reviewed his orders: Radio silence until he was twenty miles from the Port of Miami. Follow the harbormaster to his assigned offloading berth. Have all of the paperwork completed beforehand, which he'd done. Clear customs and emigrations as usual. Offload containers. Proceed up the New River. Tie her up and abandon the ship.

He reached into a satchel and pulled out the airline tickets that he would distribute to his crew. He tried to think of anything he might have overlooked. Satisfied, he picked up his binoculars and scanned the horizon.

An hour later, the captain rolled out his prayer rug and got down on his knees. Facing east towards Mecca, he recited his morning prayers. "I'll walk this day in faith, dear Lord, no foe, no storm I'll fear, but your precious word. I am safe for You are near." He raised his head, steepled his hands and proclaimed loudly, "Allah Akbar."

31

Laura and Sean's flight landed in Key West. Jesse and Rigby met them at the airport. When Jesse didn't return Laura's smile, she knew sometime was wrong. "It's my father, isn't it?"

Jesse looked down. Even though she'd rehearsed his death many times, the news staggered her. Sean had to help her to the car. They rode home searching for the right words, but afraid to speak. Finally, Jesse said, "Laura, there's something about your father's death you should know."

She sighed. "He was sick for a long time. It's for the best."

"The cops say it was a suicide," said Jesse.

Laura's voice was choked by grief. "Are you shitting me?"

"I'm sorry. What can I say?"

"Jesse, you knew my father. What do you think?"

"None of this makes any sense."

The pathway to Gordon's cottage was protected by yellow crime tape. A Monroe County Crime Investigation van blocked the driveway. Jesse parked on the street. As they got out of the car, two people exited the van. Sean held the tape up for Laura. Before she could duck underneath, someone shouted, "Stop! You can't go in there." The husky woman yelling and the man with her ran to intercept them.

Lieutenant Rita Lopez was a pear-shaped Cuban-American. She was hatchet-faced and wore no makeup. Lopez was a ten-year veteran of the Key West homicide unit. Her partner, Emler Bullet, was a victim's counselor. They played their good-cop bad-cop roles to a tee.

Rita flashed her badge and blocked the walkway. "I'm Lieutenant Lopez. This is Sergeant Bullet. We're with the sheriff's department. You are?"

"Laura Wells. I live here."

Lopez's tone was snippy. "Not tonight, you won't. This area's a crime scene. What's your connection to the deceased?"

"Gordon Wells is my father."

Bullet stepped forward. "Ms. Wells, you have my deepest sympathies."

Lopez stuck out her chin defiantly. "Like I said, you won't be sleeping here tonight."

Jesse ended the ugly stalemate. "Where was Mr. Gordon found?"

Lopez answered callously. "He hung himself in the greenhouse, as to how and why, that's still under investigation."

Bullet shook his head. Sean and Rigby turned away. Laura glared.

"My father was terminally ill. By the way, pictures are hung. Men are hanged."

"Excuse me?" Lopez appeared bewildered. She looked at her partner for support.

Laura ducked under the crime tape. "I need to grab a few things."

"I can't let you go in there." Lopez sounded adamant. She touched her holstered sidearm as a warning.

"Fine. Go ahead and shoot me."

Lopez waddled forward, but Bullet restrained her. "It's all right, lieutenant. I'll go with her."

Lopez put her hands on her ample hips. "Make it snappy and don't touch anything. You three stay here with me." Rigby and Jesse mock-surrendered by raising their hands.

The second the door closed, Laura vented. "Did anyone ever tell you, your partner's a real bitch."

"Don't pay attention to the lieutenant," Bullet said. "What about me? I gotta work with her every day. Believe it or not, she's even worse once you get to know her."

Laura couldn't help cracking a small.

Bullet followed her down the hallway. She stopped at her father's bedroom. His bed was unmade. The smell of him brought tears. Laura sat down on the edge of the bed. She held his pillow to her chest. Bullet handed her a tissue. "Ms. Wells, please don't be offended. It's my job to ask questions. Sometimes my questions can sound insensitive, but I need to uncover the truth."

"I understand."

Laura slipped into her bedroom. Bullet spoke to her from the doorway. He cautioned Laura about identifying her father's body. He advised her to send one of her friends. There wasn't a need to elaborate. Laura grabbed some clothes and was about to leave when Bullet asked, "The glass door to the hothouse was broken. Was it broken for a long time?"

"Those orchids were my father's life. Rare orchids are temperature sensitive."

"So, you're saying he would have gotten the door fixed as soon as possible."

"Yes. First of all, I don't believe my father committed suicide."

"Did your father have any enemies? Perhaps, a jilted lover."

"He didn't have an enemy in the world."

"I apologize, Ms. Wells."

"It's a little late for apologies, especially for my father." Laura stormed out of her father's house. Bullet followed her out and locked the door behind him.

The mood on Harry Rosen's Hatteras was gloomy. No one wanted to bring up Gordon's death. It was a while before Laura spoke. "Will somebody please say something?"

Jesse spoke up about what had happened. Before Gordon died, he sent two emails. Those emails implied the Arab plot was bogus. And now, there were unanswered questions surrounding his death. Jesse played the devil's advocate by raising the issue of Gordon's state of mind and the possibility of a suicide. "Maybe the pain became unbearable."

An unsettling silence fell over them as they considered Jesse's postmortem.

Laura stuck up her hand like a crossing guard at a school. "Hold it, right there. So, my father decides to end his life one day before he could talk to us. I'm sorry, but that doesn't make a bit of sense."

Jesse's lack of response meant be knew his theory was flawed. Sean shook his head in a slow disapproving way. More silence, followed by Laura's mentioning the broken hothouse door. Rigby pointed out that if her father's death was the result of foul play, everything changes.

Sean said, "I'm gonna say what we've all been thinking. Laura, as much as I respected your father, maybe he was wrong. Maybe those Arabs *are* planning an attack."

"What can we do about it?" Laura asked.

Jesse defended the CIA and he was ridiculed by Laura and Sean. The problem was they were running out of options. When Rigby asked Jesse about the possibility of getting the ATF involved, Jesse said his boss recommended that he contact the CIA.

Hearing the ambiguity in Jesse's voice, Sean said, "So, what you're saying is, like it or not, we're back to square one."

"By square one, you mean we go back to the CIA?" Laura said.

"At this point, what choice do we have?" replied Sean. "There's another option. Get the press involved. That'll get somebody's attention. Laura, if your father missed the mark on this, there's a chance he was wrong about the possibility of terrorists using the Caribbean Moon."

They looked at each other with alarm in their faces.

The discussion continued until they decided to adopt Sean's plan, which called for Rigby and him to fly back to New York the next day. If Robert Barrett gave them the runaround again, Sean would use Harry Rosen to leak a story to the press.

With time running out, Laura and Jesse decided to charter a seaplane for a quick trip to the Port of Miami. Jesse couldn't put his finger on it, but there was something about the Caribbean Moon that unnerved him.

32

Morris Ackerman was consumed by his hatred for Sean Mahoney and by his own infatuation with Sean's ex-wife, Kathy. As a serial adulterer, Ackerman preyed on a constant parade of female clients. Women in the throes of divorces were easy pickings. His affair with Kathy, had been different. She was amazingly beautiful. He was smitten. Not only did she reject him; she mocked him. His desperate telephone calls to her were unanswered. His lavish gifts were returned. Morris Ackermann was obsessed and he was teetering on a psychotic cliff.

As Ackerman drove his Bentley across the Verrazano Bridge, he reviewed his options. Sean had threatened to blackmail him. Losing a frumpy wife was one thing, losing his lifestyle was far more serious. The thought of being poor was nauseating to Ackerman.

The first order of business was to get his hands on the compromising photographs. To do this he hired the same men he sent to Key West to keep tabs on Sean Mahoney. In New York they were known as Fire and Ice. Ice was short for "ice pick", his weapon of choice. Fire's specialty was arson. They were ex-cops who got caught accepting bribes, but were exonerated on legal technicalities. The only thing between them and ten years in Sing Sing was Morris Ackerman.

Ackerman arranged a get-together at an Italian restaurant on Staten Island. He parked on a side street. They were waiting for him in a side-booth. The men stood up.

"*Buona sera.*" Fire said, "How 'bout a little vino, Mr. Ackerman?"

Ackerman eyed them with contempt. "You two bupkes fucked-up."

"How's that?" They looked mildly surprised.

"I send you to Key West to remove those wiretaps and what do you do? You blow it."

"The geezer surprised me. What was I suppose to do? Besides, it was ruled a suicide."

"I don't like screw-ups. I pay you a fortune, and this is what I get?" Ackerman opened his hands in a Yiddish gesture of dissatisfaction.

Fire and Ice bristled, but they held their tongues. Ice tried to speak but Ackerman interrupted him. "You wanna get tough with me? One telephone call and you're back behind bars. You two can double-date on the inside. I hear black inmates prefer ex-cops."

Both men stiffened. Ice gave him a blank stare and then he said, "Look, we're sorry. Hey, haven't we always done good work for you?"

Ackerman didn't disagree. He had thought about replacing them. They were incredibly brutal, which he enjoyed. And he held an ace in the hole, his threat of sending them back to prison.

Fire dipped a piece of bread in olive oil and stuffed it into his mouth. Oil ran down his chin. Ackerman handed him a napkin and pointed at his own chin.

"Trust me, whatever your problem is, we can handle it. Now, what've you got for us?" Ice said.

Ackerman described Sean Mahoney as a blackmailer. Their job was to get their hands on the photographs. Mahoney had humiliated him. It was time to settle the score.

Fire spoke out of the corner of his mouth. "So, you're sending us back to Key West?"

"That won't be necessary. Mahoney and his friend arrived here this afternoon. This is where you'll find them." He handed him a matchbook cover with Sean's Manhattan address printed on the inside.

"Now, I need the photographs. No excuses. And I want you to give that Irish prick a good beating."

Penitence painted their faces. "Hey, we're sorry 'bout that thing in Key West. Don't worry 'bout this creep. We're on top of this."

Ackerman sighed heavily. "How much?"

"Twenty grand and we'll do his brother-in-law for free." Fire unconsciously picked at the scab on his nose. He was thinking about the altercation at the marina.

Ackerman shook hands with both men and whispered, "You gotta deal."

"Thanks, Mr. Ackerman. It's been a pleasure doing business with you, as always."

"There's something else. Mahoney's ex-wife also needs an attitude adjustment."

"How bad?"

"Bad is good. Very bad is better."

"It'll cost you."

Ackerman gave him a sideways glance. "How much more?"

"Another ten."

"Done." Ackerman wagged his finger at them. "And no screw-ups, this time."

"'No muss, no fuss, no witnesses,' that's our motto."

As they watched Morris Ackerman leave the restaurant, Ice whispered under his breath, "The way he treats us ain't right, bro. One of these days, I'm gonna stab that fuckin' runt."

Fire grabbed his crotch. " I get hard just thinkin' 'bout it."

Ackerman hummed along with Otis Redding's rendition of "Satisfaction" as he drove back across the bridge to Brooklyn. He could think clearly for the first time in days. He envisioned Kathy, but this time he imagined her begging for mercy. The thought made him hot.

* * *

Ackerman's thugs spent the night parked in front of Sean's apartment building. Getting the doorman's mobile telephone number was easy. Fire impersonated a tenant on the tenth floor and asked for help with a jammed elevator door. The doorman left his post and started up the stairs.

They waited a few minutes before entering the building. They took the elevator to the second floor. Ice rang the doorbell. "Delivery, Mr. Mahoney." Sean was still half-asleep when he opened the door. They barged in just as Rigby walked into the living room. Fire stuck a .38 in Rigby's face.

"Well...well, if it ain't the limey.   Remember me, asshole?"

The kidnappers bound their victims' hands with tie-wraps. Fire led them back down the exit stairs. Ice scanned the street outside. Satisfied, he waved the "all clear" sign. They shoved Sean and Rigby into the van's side door. Ice wrapped their heads in duct tape. A split second later they were driving away on Fifth Avenue.

"Are we good or what." Fire shouted.

Instead of answering, Ice gave him a high-five.

Sean tried to memorize the turns. He guessed correctly when they crossed the Brooklyn Bridge. After that, he became disoriented and gave up.

Bedford Stuyvesant's backstreets were deserted. They pulled down a blind alley and stopped at the backdoor of an abandoned kosher meat market.

Fire unlocked the fold-up door and pulled on the chain. As the door clattered up, Ice pushed Sean and Rigby inside. They made their way around wreckage to a walk-in meat locker in the back of the store. It smelled like urine. Something scurried. Ice's flashlight exposed rats. Fire shoved Rigby and Sean into the cooler. Sean stumbled on the threshold. Rigby helped him up. The wooden floor was covered in sawdust. Meat hooks hung from the ceiling. There were blood stains on the walls.

As Ice pressed his .38 against Sean's temple, Fire strapped both men to wooden chairs. He stepped back to admire his work. "Ain't they pretty? Trussed up like two hogs waitin' to be slaughtered."

And then the beating started. The punishment lasted, until they were too winded to continue. Fire licked his knuckles. "Now, that we've got your attention. I want those photographs and the negatives." He twisted Sean's head until they were face-to-face. "You hear me?"

"Which photographs?" Sean gasped.

"Listen scumbag, you know what photographs." The sound of his fist hitting Sean made a thump. Sean's head slumped forward.

Rigby shouted, "Leave him alone. The pictures are in the bedroom closet in his apartment."

"That's more like it." Fire and Ice bumped fists.

"C'mon, let's roll," Ice said. "I'm starved. Whadayasay, we stop for breakfast?"

"You boys want something? Guess not. Don't wander off, you hear?"

Sean regained consciousness, looked at his brother-in-law and then he passed out again. Rigby heard the deadbolt drop into the lock. It was deadly quiet. The air inside was so rank, Rigby worried that the meat locker might be airtight. He chafed his face against his shoulder until he worked off the duct-tape.

"Sean, can you hear me?"

Sean mumbled incoherently.

"Try rubbing the tape off. Use your shoulder."

"It's off." Sean said.

"Are you hurt?"

"I feel like I just went fifteen rounds with Joe Frazer. They aren't gonna kill us, are they? I mean, there's no reason to kill us."

When Rigby didn't answer, Sean said, "Jesus, Rigby, I got you into this mess."

"All we can do now is stall for time," Rigby said. "They're gonna be pissed when they don't find those pictures."

"The rotten bastards work for Chang. What's so important about those stupid photographs, anyway? Unless, he wants to destroy the evidence or..."

Rigby interrupted. "You said Chang's crazy."

"He *is* crazy. Today's May the second. Hope to hell, Gordon knew what he was talking about." A moment of silence ended with, "We'd know if New York got hit, wouldn't we?"

"You would think so."

"Unless, Jesse was right, Miami's the target."

"Jesse and Laura are in Miami today."

The next few hours passed slowly. Both men fought against their bindings. Eventually, hope gave way to exhaustion. They nodded off. Sean dreamed about a nuclear attack. He saw destroyed buildings and dead bodies. He was searching for Laura digging in rubble and finding only bleached skeletons. He woke up gasping for air.

"Sean...Sean, are you all right?"

"Huh. I was dreaming." Sean tried to erase the residual image, but a vision of Laura made his heart race.

Rigby cleared his throat. "I'd give anything for a cigarette, right about now."

"Actually, I was thinking more about a crowbar," said Sean.

"Hang in there, Sean. Trust me—we'll make it outta here."

33

Every morning Gladstone waited on the same park bench in front of the Central Park Zoo facing Fifth Avenue. At precisely 7:30 a.m., an elegantly dressed man would cross the street with his golden retriever on a leash. The man would hand Gladstone a plastic bag containing yesterday's newspaper and a ten-dollar bill. Keeping his distance, Gladstone would follow the man and his dog into the park. The retriever would sniff and scratch the grass, but she always defecated in the same spot. Gladstone's job was to pick up the dog droppings using the plastic bag and deposit it in a trash barrel.

Gladstone was early. He nipped a cigarette stub between his fingernails, placed it between his lips and drew in heavily. The result was a rattling cough. He wiped his mouth and strode to the curb to spit. He noticed a van double-parked across the street. It was not an unusual sight, but there was something odd about the four men gathered around it. Gladstone ducked behind a light-post. Two of them appeared to have their hands bound behind them. The man in charge walked the captives to the street-side of the van, which blocked the view of pedestrians. Gladstone looked directly into the face of one of the men. A light of recognition flickered for a second and then faded. I know that man, he thought. Better not get involved. A barking dog startled him. He spun around and found the man and his golden retriever.

Gladstone sat down under a tree to read the sports section. As he enjoyed his first nip of the day, he thought, now, I remember you. You're that guy from Africa.

By the time, he caught up with Sergeant Mulligan, he was drunk. "I...I just witnessed a crime." His slurring was punctuated by a hiccup.

Mulligan used his nightstick to tilt back his hat. "Is that right? What kinda crime?"

"A kidnapping."

He slid the baton back into the ring on his belt. "You don't say? How much have you had to drink?"

"No more than usual. Remember when you caught me and that guy sleeping on this same bench? You dumped my liquor in the gutter."

Mulligan's expression revealed doubt. "What kinda bullshit is this?"

"C'mon, man, you gotta listen to me."

"Gladstone, I've roused you a million times. Where did this alleged kidnapping take place?"

Gladstone seemed confused by the question. "Four men came out of a fancy building over on Park... no, wait, I mean Fifth Avenue. Two were handcuffed. At least, I

[212]

think they were handcuffed. One of 'em was that same guy I just told you about."

Mulligan had a sardonic smirk pasted on his face. "I bet extraterrestrials abducted your buddy. I should run you in for makin' up such crap. You keep drinkin' that rotgut slop, you're gonna wind up crawlin' the walls in Belleview."

Mulligan's radio crackled to life. He got up and walked away.

Mulligan's disrespect stuck in Gladstone's craw. He panhandled his way back to where he'd witnessed the abduction. He was surprised to find the same van double-parked in the same place. The van was unoccupied. The emergency lights were flashing. A white Cadillac was parked behind the van.

Gladstone crossed the street and approached the Cadillac.

Jamal zipped down the window. "Yo, Pops, what's happenin'?"

"Are you waitin' for those white fellas I saw you drop off last night?"

"That's right. What of it?"

"You're wastin' your time. They was hijacked."

"Say what?" Lavon half-rolled his eyes at Jamal, who twirled his finger around his temple in a "he's crazy sign".

"If you two dumbasses think I'm lying, you can kiss my black butt."

"Lighten up, Pops, I was just jivin' with your ass."

"Jive this." Gladstone grabbed his nuts. "The men in that truck," he pointed at the double-parked van, "kidnapped your friends. I saw the whole thing go down."

"What makes you think they was snatched?"

"Cause they were handcuffed. I swear on my mama's grave."

Lavon saw two men come out of the apartment building and climb into the van.

"Thanks, Pops, we'll take it from here." Lavon handed Gladstone some money.

The paneled van pulled out into traffic. Jamal pulled out right behind it. Two black Ford Explorers followed the Cadillac.

Lavon said, "Stay on him, bro. I'm gonna call my cousin. We need muscle."

Lavon said, "Tell 'im to bring some heat."

"Damn straight."

The van turned into the alley and stopped at the rear entrance to the derelict meat market. Jamal slowed down to a crawl as he drove past. The Ford Explorers parked two blocks down the street. Minutes later, another car passed the SUVs and stopped behind Lavon's Cadillac. Four black men got out. They joined Jamal and Lavon and started walking down the alley.

Robert Barrett dialed his mobile from the lead SUV. Wick Harrington picked up on the first ring. Barrett said, "Sir, Mahoney and Croxford didn't show up. We checked out his apartment. It was empty. We followed their hired car to a deserted building in Bed-Stuy."

"Any sign of them?" Harrington asked.

"Not yet."

"What about the police?"

"Not a problem."

"What else?"

Barrett answered. "Nothing, except in another car four black men, just showed up. It looks like a Black Panther convention."

"For God's sake, don't just sit there! Find out what the hell's going on and get back to me."

The abductors saw Lavon's Cadillac drive by. They were waiting. Lavon and Jamal entered together with Lavon's cousin and three friends behind them.

"You moolies must be lost. There ain't nuttin' here to steal," Ice yelled.

"Hey, man, what about the white guys you hijacked?" Lavon yelled back.

"You boot-heads want trouble—you got it in spades," Ice sneered. Ice and Fire stepped out of the shadows with their handguns drawn but not pointed. Ice tried to say something, but his words were cut short by a shotgun blast. The first shot caused a firing frenzy. Lavon and Jamal were unarmed and ducked for cover. Fire and Ice were riddled until the shooter's guns were empty. The only sound was death-gurgling.

"Moolie that, motherfucker." Lavon's cousin shouted.

Lavon screamed at his cousin. "What the fuck have you done? I can't believe this shit."

Jamal said to Lavon, "Bro, we need to haul-ass before the pigs show."

Barrett's team was halfway down the alley when the shooting started. When the shots subsided, Barrett shouted, "Step outside with your hands up! If you have weapons, put them on the ground and back out slowly." Lavon and Jamal came out first and the shooters filed out behind them. They were all shouting at the same time, until Barrett ordered them to shut up. One of them continued to rant about his innocence until one of Barrett's men stuck a pistol in his face.

Barrett was still barking orders as he stepped outside for better reception. He called Harrington. "Sir, we got ourselves a real mess here. There was a shootout. We got dead bodies."

"Slowdown, agent, tell me exactly what happened."

Barrett described the scene to Harrington. He found Mahoney and Croxford tied up in an abandoned meat cooler. Both men had suffered beatings. Mahoney seemed dazed, but his injuries appeared superficial. Croxford had fared better. He had a medic examining them as they were speaking.

"So, the perps were the same ex-cops?"

"Yes, sir."

"Where are they now?"

"I'm looking at them. They're not going anywhere, ever."

"Other causalities?" Harrington asked.

"None. The black guys did the heavy lifting. Not a scratch. That's it."

"Any sign of New York's finest? Can you hear sirens?"

"Gunfire's more common in this part of the city than Afghanistan. Trust me—the cops won't be a problem."

"Good. Now, listen to me carefully. This is what I want you to do." Harrington's orders were to the point. Let Lavon, Jamal and their friends go, no questions asked. Move the bodies before Sean and Rigby see them. Call the police commissioner and give him a heads-up. Get Sean and Rigby to the Teterboro Airport where a private jet will fly them to Homestead.

"Anything else, before I let you go?" Harrington asked.

[216]

"How much should I tell them?"

"Don't tell them anything. One more hour, that's all we need and we're home free."

"I'll be glad when this is over," Barrett said.

"We'll all be glad. See you when I see you. Hopefully, we'll be celebrating."

34

May 2
8:30 a.m.

The Port of Miami was hectic on Monday mornings. Smoke-belching eighteen-wheelers lined up at the terminal gates anticipating payloads. More trucks waited to offload outbound freight. Gantry derricks hovered over containers like giant erector-set spiders. Ship's booms hoisted the rectangular metal boxes on decks. Railroad gondola cars carrying bulk cargo crept slowly into the port. Workers pumped diesel fuel into the bellies of ships. Forklifts and pickups scurried between the cargo-container canyons. Custom agents and their drug sniffing dogs scoured incoming freight.

Four tugboats guided a massive cruise ship into her berth between two ocean liners. She was returning from a ten-day Caribbean cruise. Her seven thousand passengers and crew members would be disembarked in less than two hours. A cleaning crew waited dockside for her arrival. Resupply trucks pulled into position.

Ships preparing to get underway added to the chaos. Buses shuttling passengers clogged the entrances and exits to the port. Stevedores loaded mountains of luggage on elevators. Stewards directed travelers to their assigned gangways. Calypso bands played. Waiters served mimosas. Ship's horns blasted.

The city of Miami was recuperating from another weekend. I-95, an artery of incivility, funneled thousands of office workers into the downtown business district surrounded by towering condominiums. Fishing guides launched their flats-boats at the 79th Street boat ramp. Sailing prams and racing catamarans sliced through the pristine waters of Biscayne Bay. The parking lot at the Miami Seaquarium was jam-packed with school buses. Mondays were reserved for fieldtrips. These activities and a million others were taking place inside of ground zero.

The Maule amphibian descended to two hundred feet east of Key Biscayne, banked left around the tip of Fisher's Island and flew down Government Cut. Laura squeezed Jesse's arm as the little plane bucked and bumped. Their pilot added twenty degrees of flaps, reduced the power and rolled in some trim. At twenty feet above the water the seaplane was still doing ninety knots. The pilot made another power reduction and pulled in another twenty degrees of flaps. The amphibian touched down as delicately as a dragonfly on a pond. Laura and Jesse cheered. The Maule taxied up to the dock at the Watson Island seaplane base.

A launch was waiting to take Laura and Jesse to the port's administration complex. Jesse and Laura jumped off the launch before the lines could be secured. They walked briskly to the building. Neither of them spoke as they got in the elevator. They exited on the fourth floor, walked down the hall, and entered the seaport director's office. A secretary motioned for them to sit down. They opted to stand. She was talking into a telephone cradled between her shoulder and neck. Her behavior suggested it was a personal call.

Jesse threw up his hands in frustration. She got the message and hung up. "Well, if it isn't agent Spooner. Thought you were still on vacation. How'd the fishing go?" She looked at Jesse and then Laura trying to make a connection.

Jesse shuffled impatiently. "I need the inbound list. I'm interested in the island freighter, Caribbean Moon. She's scheduled to dock here on Wednesday. Her last port of call was Belize."

"Oh, so this is an official visit?" She fluttered her false eyelashes. It was evident that either she knew Jesse personally or she hoped to know him that way in the future.

Jesse leaned over her desk. "For God's sake, we're in a hurry."

"Well, excu-u-use me." Her flirting melted into annoyance. She pounded the keys on her computer. "Guess what, you screwed up her arrival date. The Caribbean Moon docked here Saturday. She offloaded eight containers at 1200 hours. Her last port of call wasn't Belize, it was Guantanamo Bay."

"Are you positive?" Jesse asked.

"That's what this schedule says," the woman said. "You wanna see?"

"No. What about the location of the cargo?"

"East end, section 44, row 19. Here's the container numbers."

Jesse grabbed the list and made a dash for the door. Laura was right behind him.

"Thank you," the secretary shouted sarcastically.

On the elevator ride back down, Jesse said, "God damn it. This really sucks."

"So, Jesse, can I ask you a question?"

"Shoot."

"How many nuclear bombs have you disarmed?"

"You mean recently? Hope to hell your father was right about today's date being impossible."

"Well, if he wasn't, we're gonna know soon enough." She looked at Jesse's wristwatch.

An ear-piercing siren prevented Jesse from speaking. The port's emergency response security system had been activated. The Port of Miami was closed.

35

Hong Kong
1 minute to detonation

Throughout his life, Nelson Chang had suffered from bouts of melancholy, but nothing prepared him for the misery he was currently enduring. Even dull lighting produced mind-numbing headaches. Ordinary noises seemed so magnified, he thought his eardrums might burst. He refused to talk to anyone because their voices grated on his nerves. He had trouble sleeping. The medication that had been so effective was now useless. Chang was a prisoner to his psychosis.

Chang stared at the digital clock on his nightstand. It read 9:45 p.m., which converted to 8:45 Monday morning in Miami. He clicked on three television monitors in his stateroom. One was tuned to Al Jazeera. The second was the BBC. The third was the Chinese Television Network, CCTV. All three networks showed the same picture: a podium emblazoned with the seal of the United States and two draping American flags in the background.

Identical headlines flashed across the bottom of the screens: Stay tuned for an emergency message from the President of the United States.

The President appeared solemn as he stepped up behind the podium. The time it took a technician to adjust the President's microphone seemed like an eternity. Gooseflesh prickled Chang's arms. He shivered.

Suddenly, the lights flickered and went out. Normally, the ship's emergency generator would come online, but not this time. Chang waited in total darkness. He thought about trying to make his way topside, but decided against it. It took his bodyguards ten minutes to reach his stateroom. The second they unlocked his cabin door the lights came on. The television screens were unpictured as the global gyro antenna searched for a satellite signal.

The television monitors blinked before coming on. The press conference was winding down. The President was addressing a reporter's question. What Chang heard next increased his heart rate. He turned up the volume. The President expressed gratitude to the CIA. A major terrorist plot had been thwarted. He warned against speculating about the nationality of the perpetrators and promised a dissemination of pertinent facts in the weeks ahead. The President closed with, "And may God bless these United States of America." He stepped away from the podium. Reporters shouted more questions, which the President refused to answer. He disappeared behind a curtain.

Chang turned off the monitors. The stateroom was silent. He could hear his stomach grumbling. And then, the fear that had been lurking in the back of his mind resurfaced. He pressed the intercom next to his bed. "Did you receive any calls in the last hour?"

"I received one call from the bank."

"Think carefully, what did you tell them?"

"I didn't tell them anything. I put the call through to you, sir."

Chang closed his eye and pinched the bridge of his nose. This can't be happening, he thought. "I received no such call." He hesitated momentarily, afraid that he might be losing his mind. "Have the captain sent to my quarters immediately. And call the bank back. Make sure they didn't transfer any funds."

Chang saw the intercom light come on and picked up. "Sir, the bank says they received your authorization ten minutes ago. Three-hundred-million dollars was wire-transferred, as per your instructions."

Nothing was said, until the secretary asked, "Sir, what do you want me to do?"

"Where's my captain?" Chang asked.

"Sir, the captain was seen leaving the ship. Shall I send someone after him?"

"No. It's too late for that." Chang knew he would never see his captain again."

He picked up the pillbox on his nightstand and flung it against the wall.

36

The Lear-60 touched down at the Homestead Air Reserve Base a little after sunset. The jet taxied past darkened hangers. Four F-18 Hornets cast menacing shadows on the dimly lit ramp. A linesman riding in the back of a pickup used flashlights to direct the jet down a rarely used taxiway. When the linesman crossed his arms, the jet braked. The copilot eased down the air-stairs. Robert Barrett exited first followed by Sean and Rigby. When Sean had trouble with the stairs, Barrett and Rigby lent him their shoulders.

Barrett escorted them to the Quonset hut. Technicians were already dismantling the operational command center. They interrupted their work as Rigby and Sean were led to Hardwick Harrington's makeshift office. Rigby thought he recognized a man with buck teeth, but he lost the thought in the confusion. The workmen resumed boxing up computer terminals and disconnecting telephones.

Laura and Jesse were waiting in Harrington's office. Harrington remained seated behind his desk. When Laura saw Sean and Rigby, she gasped. Their faces were covered by ugly plum- colored bruises. Rigby's left eye was almost swollen shut. Laura and Sean held each other for a long time. "Are you sure you're all right," she whispered in an unsteady voice.

Sean held her face in his hands and looked into her eyes. "Now that I know you're safe, I couldn't be better."

She kissed him lightly on the cheek. "Let me do the talking. You read me?"

Sean's voice was barely a whisper. "Sweetheart, I read you loud and clear."

Barrett made the introductions. Before Harrington could speak, Laura took a deep breath and said, "I'd like a few minutes with my clients."

Harrington's smile was forced. "By all means, Ms. Wells, take your time. We've got lots of ground to cover. After we conclude our debriefing, the Company's aircraft is at your disposal."

Barrett and Harrington left the room. Laura said, "I can't wait to hear Harrington's take on what happened. Let him do the talking. Are we all on the same page?" The men nodded their agreement.

A few minutes later, Harrington and Barrett reappeared. Harrington stepped forward saying, "Sorry about this inconvenience. I know you've been through a lot. I arranged this meeting for a specific reason. You've witnessed a failed terrorist attack. Accordingly, you're privy to information that could affect this country's security. Caution is of the utmost importance in this situation. We must guard against creating panic. The country requires your discretion, at least for the time being. If anyone doubts me, please say so, now." They looked at each other, but didn't argue.

"Now then, Mr. Croxford, you're not an American citizen, but you *are* married to an American. And I know about your distinguished military career." Harrington looked at each of them as he spoke. "Although your service to the country can't be officially recognized, that doesn't diminish its significance."

Laura was a lawyer. Normally, she picked her words carefully, but not this time. "Cut to the chase, Harrington. My clients have been..."

"Oh, I see," Harrington said also interrupting. "This is about a lawsuit. I'd like to remind you that the United States was sued by the British government for war reparations over the War of 1812. They didn't get a dime. And may I also remind you that we rescued your friends. Sorry, I meant to say your clients."

Laura chewed her lip reflectively. "Nobody said anything about a legal action."

Harrington appeared relieved. "Did you know I worked with your father? I was stationed in Central America during my early years. I always thought of him as my mentor."

She ignored his olive branch. "I can't prove it, but I believe there are unanswered questions concerning his death."

Harrington looked momentarily shocked by her insinuation. He shook his head emphatically fending off the notion. "I'm told your father's death was a suicide." He looked at Barrett for confirmation. "He was a good man. I'm proud to have called him my friend. Did he ever mention me?"

"My father said he admired you."

Her kind words softened the hostility in the room. Harrington seemed a bit more relaxed. "Ask me any question. As long as it doesn't compromise national security, I'll tell you what I know."

Laura stared at Harrington's eyes searching for a hint of sincerity. "Okay, let's start at the beginning. Those men who confronted Mr. Croxford at the marina. They were the kidnappers. Who'd they work for?"

"Street criminals hired by Morris Ackerman to keep tabs on Mr. Mahoney. Mr. Mahoney was seen as a flight-risk. Next question?"

"All right, what about Luther James's murder?"

"James was a smalltime drug smuggler. His death was an unrelated reprisal killing as indicated by the Monroe County Sheriff's investigation."

Laura hesitated as she tried to think of her next question. "You seem to know a lot—given you people claim never to be involved in domestic snooping."

"Just..." Harrington's voice was hoarse. He cleared it with a cough and tried again. "Just because we aren't involved, doesn't mean we don't share intelligence with people who are."

"I'm curious, why didn't you tell Mr. Mahoney the truth from the start?" Laura asked.

"Public hysteria, pure and simple. As a television journalist, Mr. Mahoney created a special problem for us."

"But so much of this could have been avoided," she said.

"Long story short—what muddied the water was Morris Ackerman's obsession about the photographs. We now know he had the yacht and your father's house and Mr. Mahoney's apartment bugged. Anytime someone mentioned the Hong Kong bordello pictures, for the use of a better term, Ackerman thought they were talking about the photographs of him and Mr. Mahoney's ex-wife." Harrington looked at Sean. "Did you threaten to blackmail Ackerman with those photographs?"

The atmosphere was humiliating for Sean. He breathed out heavily and said, "At the time, I was desperate. There was only one set of pictures. I was bluffing."

Laura patted Sean's shoulder. "There's another problem. I believe my clients suffered because you delayed their rescue."

Harrington looked at Barrett for support. Barrett said, "I'm afraid, it's not quite that simple. Preventing the attack took precedence. We did what we could when we could."

Laura smiled sweetly, but her eyes were as fierce as a lion's. Before she could speak, Harrington said, "I concede that Mr. Mahoney may have been harmed by circumstances beyond our control."

"Harmed seems a bit too antiseptic, considering my client was tortured and he lost his job."

"Perhaps you're right. The government *is* willing to assist him. That's the best I can do."

Laura and Sean's thoughts were identical: he's admitting culpability or, at the very least, he's offering hush-money. Their faces registered mild surprise.

Sean blurted, "You mean you'll pay me if I keep my mouth shut. No thanks." Laura placed her hand on Sean's arm to stop him from saying more.

"No, we'll help you, because it's in this country's best interests to do so. After that, doing what's right is up to all of you." Harrington continued. "Bottom line, we prevented a terrorist attack. Everything else is secondary."

"What was Nelson Chang's role in this?" Sean asked.

"No comment." Harrington thought for a moment and then he added, "Let's just say, Chang served a purpose. That's as much as I can say."

His answer made them look at each other quizzically.

"I'm curious. Why haven't we heard more about this in the press?" Laura inquired.

She was quiet as Harrington answered, shaking her head at the voids in his story. At that moment, she realized he was stonewalling. Her eyebrows pinched together. Sean watched her with concern, but said nothing. Following several more moments of unbearable silence, Laura blurted, "So that's it?"

Sean, Rigby and Jesse worked hard not to also show their annoyance.

"What were you expecting?" Harrington asked.

Laura's voice sounded inpatient. "Well, for starters, how about the truth?"

"All right, then, Ms. Wells, why don't you tell me what you think happened?"

His sharp reaction confirmed their suspicions. They all looked at Harrington with expressions that said, "You're crazy if you think we believe you." Harrington returned a look that conveyed deception.

"What good would that do? You aren't gonna confirm what I say unless it mirrors your version." Laura felt her cheeks getting hot. It upset her to give herself away.

"I've told you the truth. It may not be what you wanted to hear, but it is the truth. I guarantee it. Better yet…," Harrington said.

Laura finished the sentence for him. "Better yet, the CIA guarantees it."

Laura thought about her father saying that a guarantee by the CIA guarantees that there is no guarantee. She stifled a yawn. "I guess there's no need for us to hang around."

They were all uneasy, especially Harrington. At last, he said, "Mr. Croxford, you're a man of few words. What's on your agenda going forward?"

"Flying back to Africa."

"Your visit has been harrowing, to say the least. I hope you'll come back and give us another chance."

"Actually, I quite enjoyed myself with the exception of the last few hours."

"Mr. Spooner, I've spoken to your superiors at ATF. I think you'll be pleasantly surprised." Jesse acknowledged his gratitude with a smile.

"And you, Mr. Mahoney, what's in your future?"

"I'm going to Africa with him," Sean said noting Rigby.

"For how long, may I ask?" Harrington asked.

"As long as it takes to finish a project," Sean said.

"Which is what?"

"Write a novel or a screenplay, I haven't decided which."

Harrington seemed concerned, but he continued. "Ms. Wells, will you be returning to your law practice in Washington?"

Before she could answer, Sean said, "She's going to Africa with me."

Harrington stood up indicating the briefing was over.

"Anything else before we go?" Laura asked.

"Not unless one of you has another question."

Sean asked the question everyone wanted answered. "So, what happens to Morris Ackerman?"

"Mr. Ackerman has made some serious enemies. I wouldn't want to be in his shoes."

Rigby raised his hand. "Any word on Nelson Chang's whereabouts?"

Barrett looked at Harrington for permission to answer, which he gave with a nod. "His yacht was seen in the Red Sea yesterday. We think he was granted political asylum by the Sudanese government."

"Hmm. So, Chang's in Africa?" Rigby's jaw tightened. Deep in thought, he drew heavily on a cigarette. When he realized everyone was staring at him, his face went blank and then the tiniest of smiles creased his mouth.

Harrington took off his glasses and waved them to emphasize his point. "Mr. Croxford, don't underestimate Nelson Chang's proclivity for violence. You need to give him a wide berth."

"If he's in Africa, maybe he's the one who should be careful." Rigby's grin broadened until it encompassed his entire face.

"You've been warned. That's all I can do." As they were about to leave, Harrington said, "Gentlemen, I'd like to speak to Ms. Wells in private."

Barrett ushered the men outside and closed the door behind him. Harrington came around from behind his desk and sat down on the couch next to Laura.

"Ms. Wells, we'll probably never see each other again. I wanted to tell you some things about your father you may not have known. My mother was married so many times I never had a real father, at least one I can remember. I was your father's operative in some very

[234]

hostile places. He saved my life more than once. In other words, your father became my father."

Laura gave him a questioning stare. Where is he going with this? she thought.

"Now, let's talk about his separation. Anytime a covert operation is compromised, by compromised, I mean innocent people get hurt, there must be a scapegoat. Is it fair? Maybe, yes. Maybe, no. But those are the rules we play by. A long time ago, your father and I were involved in a clandestine operation that went terribly wrong. Your father volunteered to fall on the proverbial sword. The grounds for his termination was fabricated by him to protect the Company from the leftwing politicos."

"So, my father was sacrificed." Laura's face turned hostile again.

"I guess, in a way. But it was his idea. You see, he believed in what he was doing. By the way, he was extremely proficient at his job."

He watched her expression soften.

"The CIA has a history of using people and then throwing them out with the garbage," Laura snapped.

"I'm afraid it's a little more complicated than that. Ever wonder why your father received full pension benefits? His length of service didn't warrant it."

She shrugged, crossed her legs and then uncrossed them.

Harrington continued, "It was payment for a career well done. In my opinion, it wasn't enough. But what's done is done."

Harrington eyed his humidor longingly.

"Ms. Wells, we're not the villains you think we are. The bad guys are the Nelson Changs in this world. Just remember, our failures are publicized and our successes

[235]

aren't recognized. Your father liked to say, 'You wanna earn medals, qualify for the Olympics. You wanna help your country, work for us.'"

Laura wiped tears away with the back of her hand. "What about my father's death?"

"We take care of our own. If your father's death was the result of foul play, we'll hunt down the perpetrator and we'll take care of business. You won't read about it in the newspapers, but I promise you, justice *will* be done. Plus, it's very good for our morale."

He looked at her and she knew he was telling the truth. They sat there silently until Laura stuck out her hand. "I must be nuts, but I believe you."

Harrington took her hand. "Have a great life, Ms. Wells."

Laura spun on her heel and strode away. As she was exiting the Quonset hut something made her glance back at Harrington. She waved goodbye and slipped into the night.

Barrett and Harrington watched the Lear rotate at the end of the runway and then disappear into some low-hanging clouds over Biscayne Bay. Within seconds, the only sound was from crickets. Harrington flipped his spent cigar butt into the weeds. He picked an errant shred of tobacco from his lip. "What's your read on our friends?"

"In what way?"

"How much do they know?"

"They know everything."

"Remember what Huxley said. 'Ye shall know the truth, and the truth shall make you mad.' The question is—can they keep their mouths shut? Three months—that's all we need."

"Sir, I'd bet my life on it," Barrett replied.

"Betting on people is usually a lost cause. This time, I think you've got it right."

Harrington fished two fresh cigars out of his breast pocket and handed one to Barrett. Lighting Barrett's cigar illuminated their faces. Barrett continued to talk, but Harrington only pretended to listen. He was thinking about Nelson Chang. By now, Chang would know that he'd been duped. The problem was Sean Mahoney had showed up at the wrong place at the wrong time. Chang would view Mahoney as an accomplice. For Chang, absolution was never an option. That would put Mahoney and his friends in harm's way. Protecting Laura Wells was paramount. He owed that much to her father.

"Bob, I'm recommending you as the new head of the Far East section."

Barrett was taken aback. "I don't know what to say, except I can't thank you enough."

"This operation has been such a resounding success, I don't see any problems with your promotion. You'll be leapfrogging some ego-maniacal back-stabbers. Watch your ass."

"It's a shame it has to be like that."

"We're like any other corporation—people clawing their way up the ladder. You need to remember that despite what the well-wishers say, they'll celebrate your failures. Just make sure your mistakes aren't too damn serious. Surround yourself with men you can trust, like I did. You'll do just fine."

"You've been a great tutor." Barrett said. "I won't forget this."

"You've earned it. Now, we have one piece of unfinished business," said Harrington.

Harrington asked Barrett to fly to Africa. It was only a matter of time before Nelson Chang would seek retribution.

Barrett was curious, why did Chang get a pass from both the Chinese and the American governments? After all, Chang was partially responsible for China's getting scammed. Harrington explained that Nelson Chang was privy to some of China's most sensitive covert operations. Chang would have taken the steps necessary to insure that if anything were to happen to him, China's dirty laundry would get aired. As an international arms dealer working for the CIA, Chang also had knowledge that could embarrass the United States. For these reasons, he was deemed untouchable by both governments. As Harrington continued to speak, Barrett realized his boss's ultimate goal. He decided against voicing his opinion. Better to keep my cards close to the vest. I learned that from the master, he thought.

37

London
Two weeks later

A rumor can travel through the financial world like a forest fire. When an anonymous blogger hinted that China's foreign accounts were caught in a major short squeeze, the stock market rallied and commodity prices plummeted. China's foreign investments were losing billions and it seemed like there was no end in sight. Hedge fund managers, circling like vultures over a dying animal, added to the illiquidity. It would take Chinese bankers months to unravel Nelson Chang's scheme to protect China's sovereign funds. The losses were incalculable.

When Chinese officials requested an audience with the U.S. Secretary of Treasury, the request was denied. The excuse given was that there was a scheduling conflict, but the real reason was to put political distance between the current administration and certain events. Instead, the meeting took place in the penthouse suite at a hotel near the Heathrow Airport in London. The men representing China worked for the Ministry of State Security, which is China's equivalent of the KGB. They wore cheap suits and matching shoes.

The man in charge of American interests was Robert Barrett, the newly appointed director of the CIA's Far East section. Two of his men worked for a counterintelligence unit within the agency. The third member of Barrett's entourage was an ex-Navy Seal. Their suits and shoes were more expensive.

The purpose of the face-to-face meeting was straightforward. Chinese investigators had learned that the three-hundred-million dollars paid to the jihadists had been electronically transferred into fifteen different banks. Those banks were overseas affiliates of a major American institution. Chinese officials asked the bank to freeze the accounts. Initially, their request was denied, but it was under review. The Chinese contended that the money was obtained by ill-gotten means and therefore it should be returned to its rightful owner, in this case, the Chinese government.

After the pleasantries, they got down to business. "I heard about your problem. What a shame." Barrett said. He looked concerned, but his tone was disingenuous.

The Chinese men eyed each other suspiciously. One of them remarked, "A most unfortunate incident."

Barrett rubbed salt into the wound. "Any estimate as to the losses?"

"The losses were very minimal. The rogue trader responsible has been arrested." The man talking looked at his colleagues for support. He mopped sweat from his forehead and discreetly wiped it on his coat sleeve.

"You don't say. We heard the losses were in the billions."

All of them shook their heads in unison.

"Another overstatement by the American press, no doubt," said the same man.

"I'm sure you're right." Barrett's expression hinted suppressed glee. "Now then, what can I do for you gentlemen? Mind if I light up?" He offered them cigars. They declined and lit cigarettes greedily. The room was instantly engulfed by smoke thick enough to cut with a knife. The ex-seal opened the window. So much smoke billowed from the window it looked like the hotel was on fire.

The delegation presented their case in a roundabout fashion, lapsing into puzzling diversions. In closing, they cited concocted legal precedents. Someone mentioned how important it was to maintain good working relations between their respective countries. The tedious presentation could have been condensed into one simple question. What about the money?

Barrett looked mystified. Nothing more was said until finally a member of the Chinese group blurted, "Sir, is it your country's intention to return our money or not?"

"Let me think about that for a minute." The silence was deafening. "I would have to say, essentially, yes, if your government agrees to the terms. You see, we *do* have a slight problem."

"Oh, what kind of a problem?" Someone inquired. "What are these terms?"

Barrett didn't pull any punches. He reviewed the failed attack and then he accused the Chinese government of knowing about that attack beforehand. The Chinese group looked stunned. They conversed in Mandarin giving their spokesman rebuttal instructions. The man speaking jumped up to make his point. "Sir, your accusation is offensive. Is your country so desperate for money that you would steal from the Chinese people?"

Barrett's face melted into rage. "Let me get this straight. My accusation is offensive and you say we stole your money. As they say in Texas, 'That dog just won't hunt.'"

Barrett's southern slang made them scratch their heads. The smallest of the Chinese men stepped forward. Barrett had picked him out as their leader from the very start. He bowed politely and said in perfect English, "Sir, please excuse my colleague's misguided allegation. If you could help us recover our money, it would be greatly appreciated."

You've tried the stick and now the carrot, Barrett thought. "That might be possible, but first things first." Barrett calmly cited the exact time of money transfers as evidence of Chinese complicity. The money in question was electronically transferred at the precise moment of the failed terrorist attack.

The Chinese defense was ballsy. They contended that the three-hundred million was actually a bribe paid to the jihadists in an effort to obtain the exact time and place of the attack. And that only the successful thwarting of the attack prevented them from warning the United States.

Barrett leaned back, placed his clasped hands behind his head and smiled, but the humor soured in a flash. The time had come to deliver the *coup de grace.* "Sir, you insult my intelligence. I know what happened and you know I know what happened. So, let's not waste time here. The perpetrators have been apprehended. As a matter of fact, they're being flown to Israel for interrogation."

There was a long intermission that grew longer. When they could no longer stand the nerve-wracking tension, the same man jumped up shouting, "Tortured men will say anything. We demand the return of this money immediately!"

Barrett unlocked his hands and leaned forward. This time, his tone of voice was irrefutable. "Gentleman, your country's participation in this unspeakable event is so reprehensible we have decided to classify the details. We suggest you do the same. If this were made public, repatriating this money would be impossible."

The Chinese representatives were speechless. Then they quarreled amongst themselves. Finally, one of them gave a half-hearted apology. It was useless. Barrett informed them that they would be contacted through appropriate channels concerning the conditions required to facilitate the release of the money. The parting was cool.

As soon as they were alone, one of Barrett's men remarked, "Sir, I think the meeting went well."

"Well enough, I suppose. It was a small victory, but any victory will do. Smug little assholes got their tits in a wringer with this one. It was gratifying watching them squirm."

Barrett went to the window and looked out. Heavy fog had settled in. It was thick enough to obscure the adjoining building. He worried that his trip to Zimbabwe might be delayed. "My ex-boss used to say the Chinese believe that if a man loses face, he loses his spirit."

One of Barrett's subordinates asked, "Think they know?"

"What difference does it make?" The distant rumble of a jet perked his interest. He cupped his ear to listen. I might get out of here after all, he thought.

"Will this slow them down?"

"In what way?" Barrett asked. He felt the need to sit down.

"Their mischief around the world."

"If it does, it'll only be temporary. I'm afraid the sleeping giant's awake. The best we can do is keep nipping at her heels. Whatdaya say we have cigars to celebrate. Don't pay attention to the labels. They're as Cuban as Castro."

"Sir, we *are* in England. I'm sure you can buy Cuban cigars at the airport duty free shop."

"They're not as good as the smuggled ones."

38

Zimbabwe, Africa

The Croxford farm appeared like a mirage. Aided by irrigation, the fields and orchards may have been weedy, but they were as green as an Irish hillside. The surrounding countryside was parched and khaki-colored. The fruit trees were budding in anticipation of the rains, but mostly they were still leafless. Laborers were back at work in the fields. Black smoke tethered to a tractor rose high above the rolling hills. Billowing clouds to the north meant the rainy season was near.

Dr. Helen Croxford's medical clinic had been burned to the ground during a rebellion. Local Africans rebuilt it on the outskirts of the Croxford farm. Africans seeking medical help arrived every day by donkey carts and bicycles, but generally they walked—some with babies lashed to their backs in crocheted shawls. They pitched tents under the jacaranda trees near the clinic.

In the morning, Helen walked to her clinic. Rigby drove off to manage the farm. Sean worked on his screenplay. Laura read books, but she felt useless. After volunteering for one day at the clinic, she was hooked. At night, they gathered on the veranda for sundowners. The fenced-in area surrounding the stone farmhouse was reserved for wildlife. They hand-fed Helen's pet cheetah and watched vervet monkeys scamper across the yard. They watched African sunsets as colorful as peacocks' tails. The air was sweet and unpolluted. It was an idyllic setting, but that was about to change.

*   *   *

Robert Barrett closed the CIA World Factbook and stared down at the Sahara desert passing beneath him. The cloudless sky was turbulent. Even at 45,000 feet the ride was bumpy. It was another three hours to touchdown at the Harare Airport followed by a four-hour drive to the Croxford farm. He reopened the book and read the following analysis:

Africa has a history of incompetent leaders, but none as inept as Zimbabwe's current president, Robert Mugabe. Once heralded as the breadbasket of Africa, Zimbabwe has been reduced to a basket-case during Mugabe's thirty-year tenure. Most of the white-owned farms have been confiscated by the government. With these farms uncultivated, the inflation rate has skyrocketed. The cost of a loaf of bread is a staggering one-hundred-trillion Zimbabwean dollars. Thirty percent of the country's black populace has fled to neighboring South Africa. The white population has dropped from three hundred thousand to an estimated forty thousand.

He rubbed his burning eyes. The plane jostled a few times and then the ride got smoother. The desert below was starting to show vegetation. Barrett scanned to a chapter entitled:

The People's Republic of China's role in Zimbabwean politics. As he read, he deduced the following: China had been a key supporter of the Mugabe regime from its inception. Zimbabwe has vast strategic mineral wealth.

So, that's the *raison d'être*, he realized.

He put the book aside. What keeps people like the Croxfords from throwing in the towel? Croxford's ancestors had been pioneers in Rhodesia. Africans were in a payback- mode caused by years of exploitation. Not sure I would've stayed, he thought.

He extracted a CIA dossier file from his briefcase entitled, The Rhodesian Bush War. Rigby Croxford, Selous Scout.

He read the following:

Selous scouts were a volunteer force. Less than twelve percent of the total applicant pool passed a selection process that was more rigorous than the SAS training course. Part of the training was a one hundred kilometer endurance march carrying sixty pounds of rocks. No sustenance was allowed except for rotten meat and rationed water. It was not unusual to have fifty candidates out of sixty quit. An ideal Scout was a mix between a soldier who could work within a unit and a loner who could think on his feet. Their purpose was the clandestine elimination of terrorists both inside and outside of the country. Their technique was to infiltrate Rhodesia's guerilla networks and set up ambushes. Belligerents were either turned into double agents or executed on the spot.

The Selous Scouts employed asymmetric warfare against the enemy which ranged from bombing private houses, abduction, M-18 Claymore mine attacks against military targets, sabotage of bridges and railways, assassinations, intimidation, blackmail, extortion and the extensive use of car bombs.

Rigby Croxford: Languages: English, Afrikaans, Shona and IsiNdebele. Expert survivalist. Skilled marksman. Demolition expert. Master parachutist. Excellent tradecraft skills. Reported to have taken part in the Nyadzonia River operation in Mozambique. 84 multi-racial Selous Scouts attacked a terrorist camp of 5000 belligerents, killing 1039, wounding 309. Scouts suffered no fatalities. Three wounded.

He stopped reading and stuffed the file into his briefcase. Croxford would make a great operative, he thought. Nelson Chang may have bitten off more than he can chew.

A liaison from the American embassy met Barrett's plane. Traveling on a diplomatic passport allowed him to bypass the usual immigration and customs slowdowns. He was whisked away in an unmarked Land Rover.

Thirty years ago, Harare was known as Salisbury. It was a prosperous city of whitewashed buildings and manicured parks. Now, the buildings were unpainted and the parks were unattended. Feral children and skinny dogs roamed the streets. Zimbabweans are known as a happy people. Their cheer had succumbed to misery.

Human conditions improved away from the city. They passed women balancing grass bundles and bags of sudza on their heads. The men carried their walking sticks. An occasional cluster of mud-huts appeared on the hillsides bordering the road. The area around huts was bare having been picked clean by scrawny goats and chickens. Children with distended bellies suspended their soccer games and waved at them as they drove past.

Halfway to the farm, they stopped to watch an elephant herd cross the road. The old matriarch blocked traffic giving her daughters and their calves time to cross. She gave them a headshake, trumpeted, and then disappeared into the underbrush.

A few kilometers later, Barrett's driver pulled over and spread a hand-drawn map over the steering wheel. "This has to be the turnoff to the Croxford farm."

The dirt road zigzagged in and around giant sandstone polyps expelled from the earth's crust and a few ancient baobabs. Croxford's farmhouse had been constructed from the same sandstone. The roof was thatched grass. A flower garden lined the walkway. Leafless teak trees guarded the perimeter.

As Barrett started to get out of the Rover, he saw a large spotted cat. He jumped back in and rolled up the window. The cat leapt up onto the hood and peered into the windscreen.

Helen Croxford yelled as she ran forward. She swatted the big cat playfully. The cheetah jumped up and placed its paws on Helen's shoulders. "Not now, you crazy cat," Helen shouted.

Barrett cracked the window open a hair.

Helen said, "You must be lost? Don't worry about her, she's harmless. I raised her..." The cat appeared to be gnawing on her leg. She stopped talking and swatted the cheetah again. The cat sulked away.

"Are you Dr. Croxford?" Barrett said, cautiously opening the door.

Before she could answer, Rigby, Laura and Sean joined her.

"Why are you here?" Sean asked.

"Why do you think?" Barrett replied. Sean shrugged as if he didn't have the faintest idea.

Laura whispered out of the corner of her mouth, "This ought to be good."

"Mr. Croxford, is there someplace we can talk?"

"Anything you want to say to me you can say in front of them."

"I apologize for my husband's dreadful manners," Helen said. "Let's go up on the veranda."

The ensuing small-talk made everyone impatient. A servant took drink orders. Barrett droned on about African politics. At last, Laura intervened. "Enlighten us, Mr. Barrett. You're not on safari. To what do we owe the honor of your visit?"

Barrett used his customary unemotional tone of voice. "Harrington sent me. There are things you don't know. I don't wanna sound like an alarmist, but all of you could be at risk."

Laura didn't hide her skepticism. "You mean the CIA lied to us. What a surprise."

"Lied is a bit strong. I prefer saying that we withheld vital information for security reasons. I'm here because my ex-boss is worried about you, and them." He noted each person.

"You don't say." The exasperation in Laura's voice hadn't vanished.

"Dr. Croxford, could I get a refill. This is gonna take me some time."

Barrett then disclosed everything, leaving no stone unturned. When they interrupted to ask questions, he answered them honestly. He left out two critical details for the end. The first was that Morris Ackerman was responsible for Laura's father's death. He stopped, giving Laura time to collect herself. She walked over to the railing where Sean consoled her. She spun back around and asked, "So, what happens to Ackerman now?"

"Morris Ackerman committed suicide two days ago."

"How did he do it?" Sean asked.

"He jumped off the Verrazano Bridge."

"He jumped?" Laura asked, her skepticism obvious.

"That's right." In spite of his best efforts to prevent it, a dry grin pinched the corners of Barrett's mouth. Sean and Rigby exchanged glances. It was evident they welcomed the news.

The second and final detail was the reason for his trip to Africa. The CIA had received intercepts indicating that Nelson Chang was making inquiries about the location of the Croxford farm. Barrett informed them that it was only a matter of time before Chang would seek retribution. He would settle the score with Sean Mahoney, who he viewed as a CIA collaborator. The people around Mahoney could be in harm's way.

"I was sent here to bring you home," Barrett said to Sean and Laura.

"You said the CIA granted immunity to Chang for security reasons. Are you trying to provoke my husband?" Helen said. "By now, I'm sure you know his history."

"That wasn't my intention." Barrett said.

"Maybe it's not your intention, but you wouldn't be unhappy if he did your dirty work."

"I'll say this much, the world wouldn't miss Nelson Chang."

Rigby stepped forward until he was face-to-face with Barrett. "Sir, I think you should go. If I decide to sort this out, you'll be the first to know."

"Are you coming with me?" Barrett said, looking at Sean and Laura.

"We're staying." Laura looked at Sean for confirmation, which she got.

"Good luck." Barrett addressed Rigby. "Oh, there's one more thing. Chang's yacht is operating around Port Sudan. He uses a different anchorage every night. Thought you'd like to know."

Their goodbyes were strained. An orange dust cloud followed Barrett's Land Rover for a long time as he drove away from the farm.

Helen put her hand on her husband's arm. "How much of that was a set-up?"

"Hard to say. I'm sure the danger's real enough. It's five days to the Sudanese border."

Laura piped up with, "Helen, can't you talk some sense into your husband?"

"In this case, I'm not sure I want to. Chang has done some despicable things here in Africa," Helen replied.

"This is my fault. I'm going with you," Sean insisted.

Rigby shook his head. "A long time ago, a woman, an American tourist to be precise, asked me if I'd ever killed an elephant. I confessed that I'd killed every living thing in Africa she could imagine, including Africans, I was embarrassed to admit. Sean, it's not like what you see in the movies. Sometimes they die slowly. What I'm trying to say is —you don't want to be a part of this. Believe me, the nightmares never end."

"It's just that I feel responsible," Sean said.

"Nelson Chang and I have been on a collision course since our ordeal in the Darfur. He caused a lot of misery. I'm not naïve. I know someone will probably take his place, but I intend to end this my way."

* * *

The following morning Rigby reviewed his plan as he drove down a seldom-used cattle path to Sibanda's village. He had broken down his rifle into four separate parts. The bolt action receiver was hidden in a spare tire. The barrel and scope were concealed in different areas in his Land Rover's chassis. The stock was buried in a tool box. He would have to cross borders to reach the Sudan. Transporting firearms was a serious crime.

Moses Sibanda was a wealthy man by African standards. He had four wives, forty cows, one hundred goats and so many children, he couldn't remember all of their names. Rigby had served with him in the Selous Scouts during the Rhodesian Bush War. Sibanda was fearless.

Rigby found him sitting under an umbrella acacia on the edge of his village. He had a small child on his lap. A herds-boy tended goats nearby. Mud-covered rondavels dotted the hillside behind him. Women huddled around cooking fires. A skinny dog barked until a girl hurled a stone at it.

"I see you, my brother," Rigby said.

"*Sakubona, Baba,*" Sibanda answered. He put the child down and pointed him in the direction of his mother. "Last night, I saw you in a dream."

"Have you been well?" Rigby asked.

"Well enough. Like you, I wait for death. My wives fight like crackling hens. There are worse things than dying."

Rigby asked him questions about his grandchildren. To delve into serious matters too soon would have been considered ill-mannered. Sibanda returned the politeness by inquiring about Rigby's family. They were silent as Sibanda rolled a cigarette as thick as a man's thumb. He spat meditatively in the dirt and said, "I dreamed about an ambush."

Instead of questioning Sibanda about his dream, Rigby told him about the threat that Nelson Chang had imposed on his family. As he spoke, he noticed Sibanda's soft brown eyes harden. He fidgeted restlessly. A distant gaze revealed his mind was elsewhere. Rigby realized the old man hadn't lost his lust for the hunt.

When he described what needed to be done, Sibanda stopped him. "Is this the arms dealer?"

"Yes."

Sibanda took a deep draw, exhaled two long plumes of smoke from his nostrils and rocked back on his heels. "Let us go now, before my wives miss me."

"The Chinaman is well-guarded. We may not return," Rigby warned.

Sibanda flashed a toothless grin. "Better to die with you than to have one of my wives find me under this tree."

39

Zimbabwe, Africa
One Month Later

INT. QUONSET HUT/ HOMESTEAD- NIGHT

Wick Harrington sits behind a metal desk. His assistant,
Robert Barrett, stands beside him. Sean, Laura, and Jesse
Spooner are seated on an overstuffed couch.
Rigby Croxford stands alone.

> LAURA   (anger rising)
> Well, for starters, how about the truth?

> HARRINGTON
> Your late father was the quintessential
> intelligence professional. He knew what we
> were up to. There was never a terrorist threat.
> The Arabs Mr. Mahoney overheard on Nelson

Chang's yacht in Hong Kong work for us. Even
the captain of his yacht was on our payroll.
We leased the freighter and the resort in Belize.
The atomic weapon was ours.

SEAN
So, the bomb Chang examined on that freighter
in Belize was fake.

HARRINGTON
In the intelligence business, things aren't
always what they seem to be.

LAURA
What was the point?

HARRINGTON
The operation had three objectives.
First, expose our security weaknesses.
Second, assess China's reliability as a
strategic partner against terrorism.
And lastly, if China acted in her own
self-interest, make them pay. That's it
in a nutshell.

SEAN
And did they, I mean pay?

HARRINGTON
Let's just say, China has had her sails trimmed.

LAURA (agitated)
Anything else before we go?

HARRINGTON
Not unless one of you has another question.

LAURA
Only one. You allege that Morris Ackerman was
responsible for my clients' abduction. That his
reason was to prevent the release of certain
compromising photographs. I submit that you
were also fearful. You were afraid my clients
might unintentionally tip-off the Chinese that
your so-called terrorist threat was a sting
operation. Keeping my clients locked up was in
your best interest.

HARRINGTON
Not so. Ms. Wells, we had nothing to
do with prolonging your clients' incarceration.
I guarantee it. Better yet, the CIA guarantees it.

Laura shakes her head in disbelief, but she doesn't
challenge Harrington.

RIGBY
Any word on Nelson Chang?

Harrington nods at Robert Barrett, giving him the go-
ahead to answer.

BARRETT
His yacht was seen in the Red Sea.
We think he was granted political asylum
by the Sudanese government.

RIGBY (grinning)
Hmm. So, Chang's in Africa. He's in my house...

FADE OUT

FADE IN

EXT. AFRICAN COAST - DAY
Series of shots
1.   An aerial of a mega-yacht anchored in a lagoon. Close up on monkeys, a lizard and colorful birds in the lush tropical jungle surrounding the lagoon.
2.   The yacht is shown from various angles until the name, Honeyguide, is seen on the stern.
3.   Close-up of Nelson Chang talking with military officers on the yacht's fantail. MOS Smartly dressed waiters are serving drinks and canapés. Armed guards stand at the railing.
4.   Another aerial shot. Pan down slowly. Two men are seen hiding in thick tropical underbrush. An unidentified man aims a rifle with a scope. The African lying next to him is using binoculars.

5.   From the sniper's POV, zero in on Chang's eye-patch. A few beats pass as the shooter adjusts his scope. The crosshairs come into focus acquiring the target.
6.   The screen darkens. A booming rifle shot is heard.

THE END

African music   Final credits

Sean scribbled the following note to Harry Rosen:

Dear Harry,

You were right. This will make a hell of a movie. You and my attorney can change the names.

All my best,
Sean

Sean tossed the screenplay aside. He got up, walked over and stood behind Laura. He put his arms around her. She leaned back against him. They looked out across the emerald highlands of Zimbabwe in the direction of the Sudan. The morning mist had been swept away by the rising sun. Cotton ball clouds drifted lazily across an aqua-marine sky. It was a beautiful day. It felt good to be alive. A brown bird fluttering above a woodland acacia caught Sean's eye. Laura handed him his field-glasses, but the bird had vanished.

They thought it might be a honeyguide, but they weren't sure.

[261]

JAMES GARDNER

JAMES GARDNER

GET THE ENTIRE SERIES!
THE ZAMBEZI VENDETTA
by
JAMES GARDNER

Rigby Croxford returns in this spine-chilling saga about the harrowing escape attempt by six American tourists caught in the middle of a bloody civil war in Africa.

JAMES GARDNER

THE BOOK THAT STARTED THIS THRILL RIDE!
THE LION KILLER
by
JAMES GARDNER

Rigby Croxford is forced into action when a tourist disappears in the Bwindi Forest. Danger follows Croxford as his search takes him from the United States to Zimbabwe to the Sudan.

More Books From Our Authors

Healing the Child Within
—Charles Whitfield, MD

**Wisdom To Know The Difference:
Core Issues in Relationships,
Recovery and Living**
—Charles Whitfield, MD

The Natural Soul
—Barbara Harris Whitfield

**Timeless Troubadours:
The Moody Blues' Music & Message**
—Charles & Barbara Whitfield

**No Accident:
Hope for Victims of Traumatic
Brain Injury and Their Families**
—Carla Christy, Mother and Nurse

JAMES GARDNER

JAMES GARDNER